Kerry Ryan Moore, once a farmer, then a soldier, a public servant and a math tutor, has now pursued diverse passions. He delves into philosophy, physics, and mathematics, finds wonder in the natural world, and cherishes his high-level rugby days. Classical music soothes his soul, while landscapes ignite his paintbrush, and narratives flow from his pen in novels and short stories.

In memory of Christopher Austin Moore.

Kerry Ryan Moore

AIN'T NOBODY PERFECT

AUSTIN MACAULEY PUBLISHERS™

LONDON • CAMBRIDGE • NEW YORK • SHARJAH

A CIP catalogue record for this title is available from the British Library.

ISBN 9781398485136 (Paperback)
ISBN 9781398485143 (ePub e-book)

www.austinmacauley.com

First Published 2024
Austin Macauley Publishers Ltd®
1 Canada Square
Canary Wharf
London
E14 5AA

Synopsis

On backwoods peninsular in South Carolina USA, where the absurd meets the darkly farcical, gather two inbred ugly wisecracking brothers – laid-off slaughterhouse men with an axe to grind. An unstable ex-army captain with a vibrating hook for a right hand who lives in a strange castle, a beautiful but disgraced cell phone and a computer hacking journalist sent to purgatory by her boss. Two over-the-top lawmen; a demented Nazi war criminal with a nemesis, a sadistic gay dominatrix, a township of throwbacks and wisecracking good old boys who want to blow up a bridge; an evil business conglomerate, man-eating crabs and at the culmination of it all; a peculiar and oddly surreal costume party and finally, to top it all off, a very big bang. Enjoy.

Part 1

Chapter 1

Tic and Tac were unusually large, crude and gloriously ugly men. Both the brothers were bald otherwise they were very hairy. Tic had an overblown soup straining walrus moustache, Tac likewise had an extra-long beard which he braided and tied down its length in three clumsy knots; all this hair was swarming with small vermin living off crumbs from Jack's Crackerjack Burgers and Chicken. Tic had a muscular condition that made his left cheek tic in time to Tac's regular clacking of the roof of his mouth with his tongue. Together, they were almost fully functioning human entities; apart, they were half-wits.

The Uglies were recently laid off slaughterhouse men from Charity Town's meat processing works in Peninsula County, South Carolina with a powerful grudge. Their positions had been within their family for generations; so the tale goes their ancestors started it all by letting their babies catch flies and eating them; their grubby little hands snatching them out of the air from their cardboard cots to the handclapping delight of their swinish parents. It was said a forebear in the US Cavalry on the trail of renegade Apache War Chief spotted him across a wide chasm and high as a kite on Locoweed and believing he could fly, he launched himself over the gap at the Indian Chief calling and bellowing – *Geronimo!* Flew all of five feet then cartwheeled into the upwards staring abyss and thus into dark oblivion.

Earlier, the American Civil War led to a belief that the men of that family were out-and-out killers, a reputation passed down through future generations. A couple of their kin in the last Battle of the Wilderness searched out and enthusiastically bayoneted the wounded and the dying of both North and South ostensibly to save them from the horrors of being burnt alive when the forests and bush lands of the battlefield caught fire. When they eventually returned minus hair and eyebrows, their bloody uniforms and boots smoking and smouldering, their Commanding Officer Colonel Fishbone who had been sipping from his brandy laced water canteen all day and was well mellowed didn't know whether to shoot them or praise them, so he threw up his hands, shrugged his shoulders and did neither.

Both Tic and Tac had the slaughtering instincts of their precedents but these were all redundant since the Meat Works cost-cutting and restructuring. The incoming owners and management, a large conglomerate had a great notion to move the Works off the Peninsular to the Mainland, although the populace suspected it was more than that. The workers were expected to move the ten miles to the new works and the township, however, the majority who hated change were fiercely resistant to moving from their beloved Peninsular. That the exercise was dooming the small shops and enterprises in the town didn't enter the Conglomerates' remorseless circuitry. The older residents likened it to the

Catastrophe of 1708, although no one could remember exactly what that was.

***

When the Meat Works was in full swing, on the Gut Floor, Fred the Works Foreman had lopped off a man's ear for sliding stuff down the wrong water-shute.

'Ya never listen to me, down the wrong sluice again,' bellowed Fiery Fred brandishing his boning knife in his usual foul mood, but all the more so as his wife had once again burnt his breakfast. In frustration, he sliced at Boo Coley; the screaming victim plucked his ear and inadvertently a kidney out of the sorting pool and ran to the clinic of Doctor Hammer, the Works Doctor.

'Sorry, ve don't do kidney transplants.' Giggled the sinister doctor, who preferred wearing a black apron like the slaughter men, rather than traditional white. The doctor's age was difficult to determine but he was definitely old and given to dying his hair blond which confused some along with his habit of abruptly standing to attention when spoken to that made the dullard management a trifle disconcerted. The doctor had gapped front teeth just like his mind and his paranoia was a slow-growing fungus within him. He began suspecting long ago that the Cockroach as he named him, the lowly office floor cleaner was behind it all and now there were many others that followed him into his ever-increasing nightmares, yet he fanatically worked on. He tried to confront the Cockroach but he always disappeared like some skeletal ghost he knew not where and the management whom he considered thick-sculled and stupid would not be drawn into the matter, no matter how hard he tried.

On a completely different level, he distributed drugs to those of the hierarchy in the know for what they called their mad mood moments and was considered indispensable. 'I am vere to look after the vorkers health and vell being,' the doctor said in his strict diction.

***

'Ah, now ee ear, that ve can do, Mr Coley.' Giggled the doctor and laid out his kit; he didn't give an anaesthetic to the injured man. 'Pain good da?' Boo almost busted his molars gritting his teeth as the doctor set to quickly and skilfully sowing back the ear and then in an act wholly unnecessary, poured iodine over the result; the scream that followed was probably heard all over Works.

'In my day, when iodine was unavailable; ve pissed on the wounds ja.'

'What say?' the patient asked in jaw-dropping shock.

'Herr Doktor Mengele at work again,' muttered Haldenstein the Cockroach as the doctor had named him who was nearby. He had a tattooed number on his arm hidden under his shirt sleeves and was busy sweeping the office floors, his daily work. Why not expose the SS doctor who had murdered his twin brother at Auschwitz? The old man was perverse; he liked seeing his sworn enemy every day. It kept his hate alive, a reason for living – and he knew the sight of him kept the doctor fearfully climbing up life's pinnacles, tiptoeing along its precipices' and apprehensively looking down into its gaping crevasses which was romancing to say the least, in point of fact Haldenstein had subtly instilled in the doctors mind the possibility of his opening the door one day, to be confronted by a tall dark stranger with a gun fitted with a silencer and Dumdum bullets.

The doctor he couldn't ascertain why, but the Cockroach made each day for him a little less certain and slowly over time made him increasingly uneasy, even paranoid. At times, he was given to breaking out in hot and cold sweats, which made his life stutter ahead slowly but relentlessly. He had chosen the Peninsular for its remoteness as a sanctuary from the Mossad as well as having meat works with a slaughterhouse, not unlike his surgery at Auschwitz and now daily he had this weedy nobody, a knobbly nemesis to contend with.

The paradox and irony of it all relieved Haldenstein of some of his own nightmares and his mental torture of the doctor gave him the satisfaction he, the Cockroach also bet the Herr Doktor was doing secret brain stem research but now he had been told he himself was dying; this changed things if he was to die before the Angel of Death would justice have been served? He thought not, and so he laid his plans and he was going to involve in it the two ugliest and most feared men in the whole of the Charity Township.

***

Doctor Hammer was an expert in sewing back different appendages. 'Ve take the day off, Mr Coley,' he muttered blearily. He had quickly hidden his nitrous oxide (laughing gas) bottle and mask he had just started using when Boo barged in. He was addicted to the gas which he also blamed on the Cockroach. Finally, the patient left, leaving the doctor strangely unfulfilled once more. He laughed uncontrollably like a Hyena then checked the corridor. *Donna und blizen there's that cockroach floor sweeper again, does he never go away?* He wanted him beaten, dead, and even eaten but lacked the henchmen like the good old bad days to do it.

Where's der gaz maske? He asked himself yawning and this time carefully locking the door before pulling back on his mask.

On arriving home, Boo's wife looked goggle-eyed at her husband's blood-soaked shirt and yellow-streaked face and turned as white as a Colgate smile.

'I know, honey, I've blood and stuff all over me, but I'm okay.'

'No no,' she screamed, 'go look in the mirror!'

So he did. At first, he could see nothing amiss, apart from the blood and the smell of iodine, and then it struck him: his ear was a ghastly yellow but what was worse, it had been sown on back to front and upside down; could this mean he could hear things half upside down or even backwards? Coley was a God-fearing ex-Mainlander – 'Now I'm part of this weird community whether I like it or not. God works in mysterious ways, He does,' he muttered miserably to himself.

The Works Manager, C J Fishbone on hearing of the incident and mellowed out thanks to a script from Dr Hammer thought for a moment then threw up his hands, shrugged his shoulders and did nothing.

Anyway, Fiery Fred the Works Foreman who had been hit with an ugly stick himself had a soft spot for Tic and Tac, they were even uglier than he was which helped his self-esteem to no end and wanted the slaughter brothers moved to the new works location but the interim management had grave concerns about letting the brothers roam the real world. The Works Manager C J also came under scrutiny and going through the staff roll with a red pen, they came across the floor sweeper and the doctor who should have been retired years ago and found to their chagrin that both had strangely watertight employment contracts until death.

Tic and Tac thought their whole family history had been belittled and betrayed and sold down Old Man River to a Conglomerate whose representatives toured the Works recently. The Reps were a team of dark-suited androgynous androids with a grey coloured ties the same colour as their personalities, no recognisable human feelings nor scruples. The robot's leader was an Asian man, Mr Chew, who wasn't afraid to get his hands dirty at the coal face to give him a modicum of credit but the ugly fact was he liked seeing his victims face to face. It brought to his normally impassive dial a smug smile on seeing his future sufferers in the flesh.

Tic and Tac had thought the takeover through and decided with their combined brains that it was near impossible to get to the Conglomerate hierarchy and decided to take their considerable wrath out on people much more accessible and while they were at it, some others, just for the fun of it. They had gone to the pub and now sat huddled together in the back bar of the Peninsula's only hotel, *the Thistle Inn*, with its ignored sign outside the front door stating: *Meat workers – no rubber boots inside – not even white ones!*

Sweet Sylvester the fat, narcissistic pub barman who considered himself roundly contoured rather than fat and was forever steeling glances of himself in the bar mirror hated the brothers Grimm, the sight of them made him nauseous, ugh. Bad for business; even though they sat in the back bar where nobody else dared to go. He made his view known to the manager. Solemn Sam, the other barman with the glum face, had no point of view on the brothers, in fact, he had no point of view on anything at all being little more than automata. The bar manager and owner, Harvard Huckleberry, was a florid-faced individual nicknamed Harvard for his phoney posh accent; he had to sit the ugly brutes somewhere out of sight and the back bar fitted the bill. Besides, Huckleberry had sniffed a rumour they may have come into money over and above their redundancy pay-outs they were splashing over his bar. So Harvard Huckleberry in answer to Sylvester's complaint patted him on the shoulder with his six-fingered hand and chirped, 'Quite the contrary, dear fellow, carry on now, all for country and money, yes sir, old chap pip-pip.'

In the present, Deputy Sheriff Just-about Early walked tentatively through the pub's bars filled with disgruntled men from the Meat Works; he pushed through the resentment and anger simmering in the smoky air; he avoided the back bar for he knew what lurked there.

Early was a bony individual forever hitching up his gun belt because of his lack of discernable hips. He remembered with morbid agony the first time he walked into the back bar of the pub and was accosted by Tic and Tac. 'Boo,' they said in unison, his first instincts were to flee. He froze, his buttocks clenched and his gun and belt fell to the floor. Oh the humiliation, he never went back to that particular bar.

Deputy Sheriff Early had been hand-picked by Sheriff Galoot Guber; a large pot-bellied bellicose man; for his computer skills, he having none himself. Just-about Early took the job for the prestige of openly carrying a gun while secretly pretending he was the famous Marshall, Wyatt Earp. The Deputy found that his main duty was to rustle up business for Sheriff Guber by actively seeking out drunks in the pub, clandestinely following them to their parked cars and radioing their licence plates ahead to the Sheriff for capture and his obligatory abuse. After checking out the pub, Early would sneakily retire and stand in the only recessed doorway nearby; the Lotto and Video Shop while he waited for Guber's victims to leave the pub. It was a horrible ordeal for him for once he was in the doorway to the radio; old Bald Maud in the shop would wink at him through the side window. She gave him goosebumps, *why couldn't she at least buy a wig? What would Wyatt Earp had done?* he constantly questioned himself.

Chapter 2

Bald Maud in the Lotto and Video Shop was backed up in the background by a brute with a baseball bat. Her boss, cross-eyed Lee Lesbone, who monitored the screen, had the lotto results flicked to Maud from his own very illegal and very sophisticated modem, usually: 'Sorry guys and dolls, better luck next time,' as he milked the system for all that it was worth. Lee was not without a sense of the ridiculous, however, and a large win on the very odd occasion was good for business and helped allay suspicion. So when looking through his two-way mirror he saw two large men come in wearing as disguise; green plastic farm buckets over their heads with slots cut out them to be able to see come furtively in to claim a prize of fifty thousand dollars, he let the charade continue and ordered his heavy to remain still. He knew these men, what a laugh. Besides, even his heavy gave them a wide berth.

Although terrified what could Maud do? The ticket was valid. Fifty grand; they would have to go to Travis city for it she said. 'No problem,' said a bucket head, the other told her they wished to remain anomalies, but Maud was almost sure it was the brothers who regularly came in to hire video nasties, mainly of ultra-violence – *The Texas Chainsaw*

Massacre, a particular favourite, followed by, *Natural Born Killers.* As it happens, the brothers didn't get much of the last movie but most documentaries are boring in parts, they reasoned but they liked that the murderous protagonists escaped justice which they equated to a swift punch to the jaw or blast from a pump action shot gun.

Chapter 3

Tic and Tac lay back in the pub's easy chairs with their blood and dung-covered boots on the low table along with their large Jack D's, pitchers of beer and laid their plans. They were drawing up a hit list.

'Put that fat fruity barman near the top of tha list, should be scooped out and used as a canoe,' cracked Tic.

'At the least, sown up inna sack and drowned,' quipped back Tac plucking at the long black chest hairs growing through the tight fabric of his ancient stained and faded chequered shirt. They were talking about Sweet Sylvester the barman, who daintily puttered about here and there. They almost ignored the old man sitting in a corner fiddling with a hearing aid and nursing a beer in his bony but very steady hands in the corner.

'Deaf as post,' exclaimed Tic glancing over at the old man and saying loudly, 'Hey old man, how's it hanging?' The old man just gaped at them dumbly while hearing every word.

'See,' said Tic.

'Wasn't he one of the Works cleaners; yes he is, Frankenstein or somethin', poor old bugger, wonder if he would like to put someone on our list? Looks like he's in need of a good deed,' said Tac with out-of-character generosity. The old man's eyes gleamed behind his droopy eyelids.

'Back to the list, place that galoot of a Sheriff at the top,' continued Tac, 'pulled me over the one time but I gave him the cross-eyed evil eye and he lit off like a cat-spooked lizard.'

Tic snatched an unwary cricket off the table and ate it. 'Walkin' peanut,' he said in satisfaction; for a couple of seconds, he was as happy as a tornado in a trailer park.

Chapter 4

The Peninsula's top cop, Sheriff Galoot Guber, was pursuing his favourite pursuit; catching drunk drivers even though he was handicapped in this regard as he had no sense of smell. His parent's doctor told them he was unusual as he had been born without olfactory glands. It was a major problem when he was growing up but to compensate his hearing was acute. It was said that he could hear the crack of a cap, the snap of a can and the squeal of a cork being pulled at a hundred yards. They also said that on the Mainland they had devices called breathalysers to detect alcohol. The sheriff scoffed, 'Smellalysers would be better.'

On one memorable occasion, he pulled over an erratic driver and commanded him to walk a straight line pointing at the road white line. The miscreant started walking then he walked faster then burst into a run, then a sprint and disappeared galloping over the rise and into the tree-lined horizon, the sheriff was so flabbergasted he never even thought of drawing his gun. When he finally did; in a fit of frustrated fury, he shot out the car's tyres and its headlights only to discover later it was stolen from a prominent Mainland businessman to whom he had to explain the unexplainable.

So now he just caught the suspects around the neck with his huge hand thrust through the car window demanding, 'Youse bin drinking?'

Guber hated alcohol. When he was six he had drunk his auntie's glass of gin and tonic, believing it to be lemonade when at a family gathering for his granddad's eightieth birthday. He drank it all and immediately felt big, strong and unafraid of all the grownups. A golden shroud enveloped him. At the large dinner table when all the family were seated, he pronounced loudly to one and all that, 'Granddad loved a good fic!' not having a clue what it meant. He was taken from the table and so thoroughly beaten on his backside that he couldn't ride his bike for a week, despite him exclaiming his granddad had said it first.

'Never never, ever drink grownups drinks again, see!' yelled his embarrassed father all blotchy and purple in the face. He heard his grandma, Nana, wailing in the background. Oh, he saw alright.

In his teens, he was escorting his beloved Nana who could see no wrong in him to the Lotto shop, his frail grandmother muttering and clutching a rumpled ticket to her bird-like chest, 'I've got it,' as she had many times before; this day dreaming about Paris, Venice and chiffon, she stepped off the footpath. The drunken man-boy in his souped-up car doing power drifts and slides never saw the pencil-like figure till too late. The ticket whisked down a drain. The killer driver was never apprehended nor was the million-dollar lotto prize claimed. Oh, Guber saw alright.

Chapter 5

At an emergency Council meeting of Charity, there had been emergency meetings previously with the Meat Works move top of the agenda but nothing had been decided, no plans laid, no action taken; it was all too hard to get their heads around. They were so demoralised by events the subject was eventually taken off the agenda as if the problem had been solved. The perennial subject of the town's Sheriff came up.

A councillor said in her high squeaky voice, 'The Sheriffs a disgrace.'

The Mayor Otis Botox Clone who had a severely lined brow that nothing permanent could iron out was more depressed over the move than most; his position was on the line. 'You people keep forgetting the street brawls, general thievery, the assaults on females and the road toll before Guber took over.'

'Yeah,' muttered a Councillor, 'now all the violence is committed by the Sheriff.'

'Or inna confines of peoples boozy shacks,' drawled another.

There was an embarrassing silence.

'Moving on,' said Mayor finally, 'what we are here for, what to do about that large road crater?'

'Subsidence,' interjected a further Councillor wriggly his striped back curtsey of Gloria the town's dominatrix further into his chair.

'At Hope Beach,' continued the Mayor unfazed slowly easing his burning buttocks back into his chair, 'and the tossing of refuse off Charity Point.'

Chapter 6

The Man on the Hill climbed out of his pit of apathy and laid back his large telescope on its tripod. He had been looking at the only multi-storied building in Charity, an ancient relinquished church. Why it was first abandoned was as obscure as its founding. The ground floor it was said had been used for devotionals, the second a communal sleeping area and above all, an extremely large and peculiar square bell tower, minus its bell which had been melted down for money in harder times. More recently, the church had been converted, the rear housed a vehicle workshop while the front half with its tower, housed the Peninsular Advocate the Counties weekly newspaper; its ground floor cluttered by an old-fashioned printing press and filing cabinets, the second offices and the third, the bell tower itself, was converted into two compact self-contained apartments. The old church had been superseded by a clap-boarded evangelistic church styling itself, God and Co Inc. The Man on the Hill had been focussing on a very pretty woman with red hair who had just disappeared into the old church.

Captain Rickard Hook the Man on the Hill sat back down on his favourite chair once again with the family chronicles, Peninsular history and plans of the Castle though in no particular order and lay in a messy heap beside his chair. He had retrieved them all from the back of the mansion wine cellar. To call it a mansion was a misnomer, it was more a kin to a Scottish Castle with its battlements of solid stone than a palladium collonaded fronted Southern American classic; which he wished it was, he thought the Castle grotesque, he could hardly bear to live in it. Also deciphering the slabs of paper with its oldie English penmanship was brain busting; there was some modern stuff mixed up with the old, including his own father's, with whom he had had a complicated relationship. His writing declared the Korean War just almighty and he didn't buy there being two Koreas; there was one too many as it was. Now thought the Captain if only he had an intelligent and willing helper to sort and edit this unholy mess; a mission, it had to be someone he could trust but he procrastinated, as usual, something he excelled at. He had another mission that involved the takeover Conglomerate whom he called the Big Con. 'Oh Pappy, so brave,' he reflected sentimentally. He was reading a short report of one of his father's deeds while in Korea.

The guys at Rear Base X were having a game of football, a tall guy as a wide receiver went tearing off backwards trying to catch a throw, he felt a wire at the back of his legs, it snapped with a rusty plunk and he kept stumbling backwards.

'Mine!' he had cried.

So did all the men. 'Mines!' they screeched.

He froze. The football continued, bounced behind him and set off an anti-personal mine. Dust and stones flew up and around, a piece of shrapnel removed his cap, and another zipped past his ear. He stood there frozen in shock in a cloud of settling dust and dispersing the smoke. Major Hook already a World War II Vet took unthinking action, he retraced the man's steps, picked up the stiff soldier's body in a fireman's lift and carried him back the way they had come.

'You almost got it,' was all the Major said when he got his breath back and looked back at the minefield protecting the camp's perimeter.

Captain Hook recalled his quiet homecoming from Afghanistan. His once domineering but now frail father met him alone at the front door, his mother having been long buried. 'My son, my hero,' the old man spluttered, then eying his son's Purple Heart, campaign medals and other chest candy on his uniform jacket, fell forward dead in his arms. The funeral was a solemn affair with a few attendees. At the church service, a Korean veteran, tall, shaky and grey as an old fence post tottered forward to give the final tribute.

Holding the sides of the pulpit with a grip of iron, he looked into the far distance as if steeling himself then. 'Major Hook saved my life,' he proclaimed in a surprisingly loud voice and pulling the pulpit with him toppled backwards dead as a piece of driftwood. All in all reflected the Man on the Hill, not the happy homecoming he was expecting.

The next morning he was once more back at his spyglass that was one of his pastimes, the others were occasional golf, drinking and being spoiled by his small staff of three. He was observing a vision in the window of the large bell tower below a pink leotard-clad young female body was in a room launching herself into a series of somersaults and pinwheels through the air towards the window, red hair tossing back and forth, ending with a scissor-like movement of the legs and a twist. *Was she an acrobat, gymnast or something?* To his delight, her series of exercises seem to run on forever; the downside was it made him feel like a dirty old man. He was twenty-five.

Below in the township, Serena Pussyfoot finished her Chinese classic wrestling move called *the Flying Scissor Snap*. What was that flashing up on the hill? The sun off a car windscreen or a window? Ha-ha, Morse code? Stopped now. She moved away from the window and peeled off her leotards, readying herself for work. Wrapping a towel about herself she stepped into the bathroom for a morning shower. She smiled grimly to herself, something was moving behind a peephole, she had discovered under the wall mirror. Stealthily, she slid under the hole, took a pepper spray canister from a shelf, shook it, then reached across and sprayed the nozzle directly into the hole. An ungodly scream screeched through the other side of the wall, followed by deep sobbing.

Serena arrived down for work dressed in a sombre trouser suit, a prim blouse and had tied her red hair back in a granny bun. Previously, on her arrival at Charity, she had stepped off the Greyhound Bus into a red mini-skirt, matching boots and a low-cut tee shirt, her red hair with a yellow ribbon tied in a ponytail flashing and flaming behind her. Chief Bluebluff, the Peninsula's token Indian went spook eyed and as did his horse high kick, which ran through the window of the local florists where it began to eat the roses.

Serena had made her way down from her apartment to the Newspaper office below and entered its grubby foyer.

'God!' she exclaimed to herself looking about in disgust as she made her way to the reception desk. A spider-like man called Sidney Stilton with a mouth full of snaggled teeth greeted her again.

'See you well settled into your apartment, Miss Pussyfoot, then ever?' he said with a leer, which he mistakenly thought was a smile. She nodded.

'Well now, we better take you to the boss. This way,' he said and led the way down a long corridor with a couple of large cubicles on each side. 'Number two is yours,' and knocked on a door at the end stating Editor in fake brass lettering and opened it. She went in. Rising from a plastic desk was a small red-faced man with overly large earlobes and an equally large black eye patch.

'Temporary inconvenience,' he said with a grimace, his one good eye squinting at her while nervously pulling at his lobes. 'Rose pruning, a thorn,' pointing out the patch over his right eye and reaching out his paw. She took it. It was limp as a dead fish. 'Ah Miss Pussycat, welcome to our humble rag.'

'That's Pussyfoot, Mr?'

'Lowell, but you can call me Larryoe, ever.'

'I see,' replied Serena. 'Mr Lowell. You are probably well aware I'm not here by choice.'

The horrible truth was that she had been banished to this off-the-map place. She had been set up by her own vanity. She had worked for a big city newspaper and was considered a real hot shot with prospects. When the Editor-in-Chief went to attend a conference of a conglomerate of papers for a week, he left smirking and full of himself. 'Something big going down. They say even Murdock maybe there, how about that!'

He left the paper in charge of Sub-Editor Carrington who had a love-hate relationship with Serena ever since she turned him down for a date; to regain impetus, he looked at her. 'Get me something real spicy while dickheads away,' he said as a challenge. She accordingly hacked into some celebrities' lives but thought them boringly facile. However, after more than enough cocktails, made up a short but spicy story and wrote it up just to spite him. And to her utter horror, the temporary brain drained Carrington ran it.

Senator's Wife's Lab Experiments, ran the headline on page three. Followed by: *The Senator's wife and friend's unusual love of their Labrador dogs...*

When the Editor-in-Chief returned to be greeted by the third-page headline and content, he went ballistic, fired Carrington on the spot for unprofessional conduct and had Sarah stand at attention in front of him. 'Sarah, ya a flipping lunatic of some kind?' he cried. He was fazed, he had begun to fancy this woman.

She took umbrage; asking if she was a madwoman, what next? 'You can't,' she almost bellowed.

'What do you mean I can't?'

'You've been molesting me in the workplace. I have witnesses, remember the article in this very paper: Woman receives million for sexual harassment.'

The Editor's face darkened. 'Well, you can't stay here that's for damned sure.' He pondered some more pulling on his over long ear lobes. 'How did you get your information, straight up now?'

'Some very mild hacking and er other stuff,' she said trying to cover her tracks and inadvertently plunging herself deeper into the mire.

'Don't tell me about no other stuff! Good grief, that was what the damn dumb conference was all about, hacking and stuff. We're both stuffed and you are going to be lynched stuff it.'

It was a real pity, he erroneously felt sure there was something going on between them. She reminded him of Nicole Kidman; he pretended to deliberate some more, pulling and stretching his earlobes.

'This is what we must do, most of the blame goes on Carrington's shoulders with you a close second. You're an untouchable, probably a criminal. You're to depart under a pseudonym. Forwarding address unknown, return unlikely.'

'But I never thought the idiot would print it…'

'But he did so, so no buts. This is the deal, take it or sizzle alongside me.' Actually, he probably wouldn't, he had two scapegoats and his out-of-town alibi. 'I'm sending you to hide out at my cousin's paper at Charity for a while, he owes me.'

'Where's Charity? What about salary?'

'Charity's a town on a largest peninsular in South Carolina, nowhere no place really. Called Peninsular County, a huge spit of land. Charity's is a one-horse town with a donkey for a Sheriff.' He laughed with a snort. 'Speak funny peculiar, for instance, they add the word *ever* to every second sentence short for whatever, I guess but I digress.' He snickered. 'Now then, same salary, drop the molestation crap. Disappear, change your name, see you in about six months,' he said slumping back in his chair with his arms behind his head whistling Dixie.

Sarah Parsons looked down at the black triangular-shaped toe of her shoe and muttered, 'Lord grant me serenity.' 'My new name is Serena Pussyfoot,' she said as she turned and abruptly left with her head held high.

Chapter 7

Mr Lowell owner editor of the Peninsular Advocate held out the phone from his ear from *the voice*. 'Treat her real nice or I will feed your gonads to my Doberman. Clean up that other apartment in that silly bell tower next to yours, put in all the mod cons, bill me directly see.'

'There's a guy already…'

'Kick the hick out. Start setting up today, now in fact. Keep her occupied. No questions, I'll be paying her through your office fortnightly, bye.'

Mr Lowell sighed, his cousin was such a bully, he called Peninsular County with derision Spittoon County but he did set up this newspaper for him, if only he suspected for his own amusement and in return, he had given his big city cousin the Crab Thing.

From above Lowell, Selena stepped out of her apartment and descended to the second-floor offices and started proofreading advertisements, personals and the death column. 'The latter is your column,' said Editor Lowell, previously the first day she was there as if he was giving her the White House. Mr Lowell passed by.

'Nice day Mr Lowell,' she called. Lowell placed a finger between his new neck brace and his throat and painfully wriggled it.

'Ya ya ever,' he replied trying not to catch her eyes with his one. 'It was only in fun,' he muttered to himself, 'no sense of humour, this woman.' He could not help himself. Her very name aroused him. He thought he was being witty by her calling her Miss Pussypaw, Miss Pussycat and Pussypat. His mind game came to an abrupt end in the corridor the other morning when he called out to her approaching form by calling out cheerfully, 'Morning Miss Pussycute.' Suddenly, she was somersaulting towards him and then her legs were wrapped vigorously around his neck. He had a nano second of ecstasy seen, then his head was violently snapped to the side and he fell to the floor, writhing in agony. *What had his cousin landed him with? Wonder Woman?*

'You're to wear the neck brace for three months, you're just short of a broken neck,' said his doctor not believing for a moment that his patient had fallen out of a golf cart.

Chapter 8

Captain Hook sighed, *time for a drink. Too early true, but another day to endure.* He marched down the hall to the secret door leading to the wine cellar swinging his hook and brushing his left hand through his blond crew cut. It was the darnest thing he mused; Afghanistan, Kabul, bloody Afghanistan. Damn his family's insane obsession with its male members going off to war to prove themselves in their father's eyes; gambling their lives in fact, chest candy, torment and death. Consecutive fathers through the ages had said: you boys got to earn it, meaning the inheritance of multimillions and the large estate. It was all incomprehensible; an inherent madness. His elder and only brother died in Iraq when a crazed screaming stick figure burst through some smoking and burning oil and turned him into a colander with an AK47. For himself, if he ever had a son, he would never send him off to war, be it in Antarctica, Mars or inner or outer Mongolia or right here in the good old US of A.

On his very first tour of Afghanistan, he was leading a patrol out front as a lieutenant. He was nervously spaced out and with his home South Carolina on his mind he saw a splash of green and red against the grey and dun-coloured desert. Approaching closer and looking down, he was surprised to see a small kewpie doll. *Was it a lucky charm a previous patrolman had lost out of his pack?* He bent down, picked it up and it promptly blew his right hand off. He explained to his Commanding Officer at the MASH unit, 'I picked it up to spare my men from danger. I meant to throw it away out of harm's way, sir.' The Commanding Officer studied the report in front of him. He pushed back his cap and scratched his head. A gallantry award crossed his mind but briefly.

'For your pension, I'm promoting you to captain,' said the Colonel unaware of Hood's wealth, 'awarding a Purple Heart and sending you Stateside, dismiss.' Lieutenant Hook now a captain rested from lying to attention in his bed as his CO smoking a cigar slouched out of the tent flaps shaking his head.

On returning home, the military, with his consent gave the Captain an experimental prosthesis made of silicone, rubber and plastic hooked up to nerve endings in his arm and wiring to his brain. By concentrating, he could open and close the hand, pick up things, albeit slowly as it required concentrated mind power. He liked it so much that one late afternoon, mostly drunk, feeling down, very low and alone watching the Playboy channel, he found himself masturbating with it. It was fine for a while though a trifle impersonal, when something went horribly wrong, the hand would not stop, and he was being worn away. He ran around the room screaming in agony. He tore the hand and its wires, clamps and other connections from his arm and head and dumped it all down the toilet where it made a sizzling sound before dying and called the Mainland ambulance blathering in pain and self-disgust. The ambulance team looked at CAT (Crisis Action Team) who dealt mostly with potential suicides and stuff like that in their white coveralls leaning against their car illicitly smoking.

'Hey guys, may have a weirdo, happy days, follow us to the scene you could see some action.' The paramedical CAT team were grateful; they hadn't had a call out in a week and they were bored stiff. The last one was to the Peninsular as usual; a woman rang dispatch hysterically screaming that her husband had gone barking mad.

'We better take a dog net,' said the driver to his buddy as they took off. They found the husband naked on all fours cocking a leg at the kitchen table, and an empty bourbon bottle lay on the fore mentioned. 'Told you we should have brought a net,' said the driver watching his buddy readying a syringe.

On this new mission, two vehicles took off sirens screeching from the Mainland to the Peninsular and the Castle. Painted on the side of the CAT car were the words Mercy Mental Hospital. The Captain was taken in the ambulance to the Mercy *Medical* Hospital under heavy sedation. Manhandle, one of his staff at the gate baffled barely had time to wave goodbye. The Hospital staff are still laughing about it to this day. But the CAT car was noted by some of the towns and the Captain summary declared the Loony on the Hill. He now had a hollow lightweight stainless steel hook affair with an almost finger-like point at the end so he couldn't hurt himself or anyone else. The hook although clumsy in the beginning, he could now manipulate with dexterity and without fear. He had an electrical technician make a roundish cap on the end of the hook and insert an oscillator and batteries to make it vibrate and thus instead of stirring the sugar into his tea or coffee, he just placed his hook into the cup and vibrated it; it amused his few visitors. He thought of 007, *to hell with both shaking and stirring.*

Captain Hook continued his stride down the hall, at twenty steps he stopped and opened the hidden cellar door, turned on the lights and descended the steps into the cellar. Revealed were hundreds of square feet of wine bottles, many of venerable vintage, all worth a small fortune. He picked out a special champagne, a French aristocrat and carefully wiped it clean. In a far corner was a large open crate of Scotch single malt whiskey which he never really liked despite his Scottish ancestry. He cradled the bottle of wine; he knew the history of this particular bottle. His great grandfather had liberated it from under the French Marshalls contingents' very nose when as Colonel Hook and adjutant to the American General with the Allies, were celebrating in the railway carriage after they accepted the Germans' 1918 surrender. Outside the carriage, after the Germans had left he had relieved a surprised sergeant come waiter of his burden. The veteran sergeant did a smart about turn and marched off and fetched another bottle without so much as a blink of his stoic eyes. This very bottle was the start of the vast collection before him. *So what*, he thought irreverently, *here today, more gone tomorrow,* he reflected, pop. He didn't do much all day except trawl through the archival stuff from the cellar. He found in the detritus some papers with an anchor on it. 'Ah ha,' he muttered, a connection to the only Hook to become a sailor rather than a soldier and in the Civil War and nearly at war's end with no Rebel Navy to speak of was promoted to Commodore. The Captain felt some empathy with this rebel and he read the mangled manuscript avidly and went to bed early and dreamt of Treasure Island, pirates and other cutthroats and then a terrifying nightmare in which he was forced to walk the plank by his father of all people.

***

Out to sea below the castle, a thick white-grey fog bank was heading into shore as a slow-moving avalanche began smearing the outskirts of town. The fog was backlit in primrose as the sun struggled up out of its bed as had the Captain. As usual Marie, a pretty olive-skinned woman and his full-time cook had laid out his breakfast of ham and eggs. After breakfast, he continued with the archives, he was particularly interested in the period 1708 or thereabouts, whereby a catastrophe had taken place, what it was he had no idea, *a plague, famine, a war?* There was also the matter of the very large missing wing to the castle: he had seen it on the old plans from the cellar; surely the two events were connected. His highly reticent family were firmly silent on both subjects and they were about most things important and glossed over or ignored his questions even as he grew into a man.

When on the odd occasion, he had driven through the town he had a feeling of Deja-Vu, a stone wall here, cottages there, a building of stone across a street and incongruently, a large stained glass window depicting a heraldic crown over a stylised Scottish thistle at the pub's entry, all obviously from the Castle wing for the rebuild of the town.

Outside, he sat in his favourite chair musing and taking in his estate. Where the slope flattened out stood the guardhouse come to keep with its own quarters, kitchen and so forth. The stone building was surrounded by a cast iron palisade of pikes strong enough to stop a rioting mob or say; a small siege army. Over the modernish scrolled metal gate leading to the castle was the motto, *Fortuna Juvat*, below a thistle crest.

He thought that he could just as well be a man of total leisure, a Lotus Eater in the Bahamas, the South of France, Monaco, or the especially South Pacific. He could write a book, a history of his family and the Penisular as a legacy, paint a picture ah la Gauguin though he had a talent for neither, but he could try he thought, he had the leisure and finances that conquered just about every obstacle. Most of his vast inherited fortune lay in a secret account in Zurich Switzerland. Where ever he lived it would be in style and comfort, it was idiotic to stay. Of course, it was mostly for the solitude, he reasoned then argued to himself but not very convincingly. He liked the majority of the town's folk, they were weird but his people. He was also fond of his staff; especially Manhandle the keep and gateman come almost everything, factom come something. Manhandle was always full of good-humoured advice, especially on the Castle's golf course whenever the Captain had a poor round. The golf course also served as a landing area for a helicopter or small aircraft. So there was Marie his cook who never put a dish in front of him he didn't like and the brown round-eyed Millie, the wiry and strong willing helper in everything that was done inside the Castle and of course, the indispensable Manhandle. He knew for a fact he was spoiled rotten and guiltily hung this fact about his neck like some sort of sin. *Why did everything have a flip side?* He remained baffled by what he thought was a deep philosophical question.

Chapter 9

Selena stepped out of the Advocate Building for lunch. It was a warm but hazy day, a froth of sea fog had made it inland and the buildings along the main street appeared almost ghostly. Here and there indistinct figures walked through the gloom. *So Jack the Ripperish,* she thought. Ahead of her two bald-headed sasquatches came out of a door carrying large cartons of beer, one gave a high-pitched wolf whistle. The other gave a short but wild rebel yell that froze her spine. She abruptly crossed the road to the sanctuary of a takeaway shop opposite. Wouldn't you know it; two monsters wallowing in the fog, their type of Southern Hospitality she didn't need.

A pug-nosed, bare-footed, snaggled-toothed man wearing a battered black motorbike helmet, a badly stained singlet and shorts grinned at her while doing a grotesque gig alongside the shop. Ugh, fear and dread. Safely inside, she asked what or who was that outside?

'Oh, that's just Road Kill Billy you could fit his brain in a walnut shell, gone now, 'armless, he only eats road kill, hogs, dogs, boids, coon loons; stews them all up they say. Well, it don't set well with me, have to tell ya, me serving food. Real unappetising but now, whatever *you* wants, welcome ever?' she spewed out. *Did everyone here give to wisecracking?* she thought.

'He wears the helmet against folk throwing rocks at 'im to drive him outta town,' she added as an afterthought.

In an almost reflex action, Serena pointed at a ham on rye sandwich in a cabinet. The girl behind the counter with cross eyes and a sharply receding chin took her order and gave it over, sneering, commenting it was a lovely day ever. Serena came to the conclusion that the sneer was a permanent disfigurement. This whole county was surreal, she was sure she could hear a banjo plunking somewhere; she had never met or seen so many knuckle draggers concentrated in one place bar none *ever,* she drawled to herself, *good Gawd am beginin' ta talk like them in me hed ever,* she thought.

Chapter 10

Tic and Tac weaved their way to their ancient Chevy pickup, turned on its large fog lights and drove home with their cartons of beer to their place called Lone Oak for its century's old oak growing at the front gate along with a letterbox that had fallen off its post and now lay neglected on the side of the fenced access road. The property itself was a bits and pieces affair. The original homestead had been burnt down during the Civil War and now all alone, a stone chimney made a rude gesture up towards the usual high blue sky. Originally the largest farm, but bit by bit sold by generation after generation the remaining land had mostly if slowly reverted back to an oozy bog till all that remained was a large fenced grassed paddock on a hillock, a big old barn and a substantial hog pen at the back containing pigs and piglets. Turkeys gobbled as well in the paddock with its creek running a murky channel through it. The turkeys were for Thanksgiving and Peninsular Day, whereby the animals lived on the moods, whims and appetites of the brothers. Usually, they sold the majority to the Works, another bone of contention for them to gnaw on now it was closing. The access road led directly to the old large barn that was their home. Their living area within the barn with its rough concrete floor consisted of two bedrooms, a kitchen dining area and a large lounge. The toilet at the rear was an indoor outhouse over a long drop hidden by a full-length tarpaulin curtain across the width of the barn. Also behind the tarp was a large slaughter area with all the paraphernalia associated with the process. The heating was via a large gas burner with a side plate for barbequing. With part of their recent Lotto winnings, they bought a replacement 4x4 vehicle, a new wide view HDTV, a new DVD player, plenty of chicken, reclining chairs, another large fridge and a shiny galvanised steel water trough. The brothers reclined in their Lazyboys and snapped open a couple of beers. Tic opened the ledger and the list.

'Hey, ten already.'

'Not bad going for two days work ya,' replied Tac delightedly. 'Did we need ta bag more what ya say, Tic?' he drawled trying to twirl his moustache without much success.

'Nah, more than enough and it would be best to herd them all together,' replied Tic picking at his sharply receding chin through his beard.

They sat thinking, gulping their beer and smoking up a smog.

'Brain hurricane,' yelled Tic, 'a party.'

'Hey, that will work, but how?'

They got more beer and opened a Jack D to help them think more clearly. A half-hour later, they had the solution.

'We invite 'em here,' said Tac rubbing his hands gleefully.

'Yeah, holy smoke, we send out invites,' replied Tic copying Tac and rubbing his own hands. 'With sweeteners, inducements, free food and booze. Who's gonna resist? Ya know this greedy lot, especially the bosses, they get a sniff of something free and they'll crawl halfer mile over broken glass just to *see* it.'

'Decorations, dancing gals; well maybe not. Straw bales for tables and chairs. Coloured lights; eeha,' bellowed Tic in a delirium of joy gulping bourbon from the bottle and passing it to Tac.

'All thanks to Lotto, they oughter hava Lotto church where ya go to give thanks,' concluded Tac.

'Pass the Jack back, Tac, haw-haw,' haw-hawed Tic.

'Hee-hee,' hee-heed Tac, 'we're on a roll, what gear do we need?'

'Um, rope. That big old electric chainsaw, the extension cords a bit iffy but don't matter handcuffs,' said Tic.

'And clubs. Hey, let's call it a costume party, ya know, a fancy dress party,' contributed Tac.

'Brilliant!' they both breathlessly exclaimed.

A long silence followed while they smoked and drank, then, 'What do we hang them all on? We only have the one hook.' They pondered a bit longer on this thorny problem and other things but their brains fused and they both fell into a coma-like sleep. They awoke still in their chairs, stiff and hung-over the next morning. Dozens of empty beer cans, cigarette butts and a mostly empty bottle of bourbon littered the floor. Tac groaned and being his turn retrieved some chicken pieces from the icebox and slapped them on the gas griddle and lit a smoke and had a coughing fit. His protruding a pale blue eye like his brother's, started from his head and then popped back.

Tic staggered out to the toilet and coming back, pushed aside the tarp and kicked a path through beer cans, muttering and groaning. By the time he returned to his seat, some chicken breasts and drumsticks were sizzling on the griddle.

'I would 'ant go back there's awhiles, let off enough gas to inflate the Goodyear Blimp.'

'Do ya remember anything from last night?' questioned Tac with his breath back and having turned the chicken served them both.

'Every good word, my bad man, hee-hee,' replied Tic leaving his chair and getting more beer for them to wash down the food.

'Solved the hook problem, damned obvious, don't know why we didn't figger last night,' announced Tac.

'The Works?' guessed Tic his head clearing as he pared his hornlike fingernails with a handy butcher's knife.

'Yeah, we just go over yonder and get 'em, them guards are as useless as a chocolate coffee pot, don't know why we got all up fussed about.'

The security guards did not worry them the slightest; they would take along their baseball bats just in case for the stupid. The guards were a small team patrolling the vast premises guarding against vandalism, pyromaniacs and among others, thieves, who given half the chance would have stripped out all the valuable lead and copper piping including the tons of brass. Tac gave a hog-like grunt, 'Let's go to the pub, I think better there.'

'Now you're talking some,' replied Tic.

There was a rap-rap on the barn door. Tic looked at Tac who picked up a nearby pitchfork.

'Who's there?'

'Ooh ooh, Cousin Leroy,' came back the hesitant reply.

Tic edged up to the door and looked through a gap. There stood a man of about twenty-five, skinny, tallish, wearing faded blue bib overalls over a reddish tee shirt and fake black leather, silver chained jacket over all that. His blonde hair was strung into dreadlocks long, thick and greasy looking.

'Boy, did I get a good deal for youse guys!' he shouted through the gap. Tic threw the bar off the door to let him in. Leroy stood there bandy-legged.

'Come in, ya idiot,' said one of the brothers, 'take a seat,' pointing to a hay bale.

'What's the deal, mule breath?' grunted Tic.

'Got the word y'all struck it good – got it through Ugly Auntie,' he said with a wink.

'Have a drink,' said Tac ignoring Leroy's wink and passing him the last of the bottle of bourbon.

'Most gracious guys,' said Leroy taking the bottle, drinking deeply and nervously, sucking out the last of the dregs.

'So ya still dealing drugs,' said Tic sneering and looking at Leroy's hair in distaste.

'It's a living, family to support meaning mainly me that's why I'm here see, with your order,' Leroy replied defensively.

'Seeing you've drunk the last of our booze, we're fixin' to go to the pub.'

'Can't we deal here?' whined Leroy who had a phobia about public places.

'No,' said the brothers once again together. 'Ya follow us ata distance, be in the back bar. On arrival, ya wait at least ten minutes before coming in.'

'My car is a rare purple Charger, a classic,' said Leroy said trying to gain prestige with the two heavies.

'So,' replied Tac, leading the way outside and stripping the tarpaulin from their new huge black 4x4 Bruiser with multiple gun racks fore and aft and covered with enough bull bars to hold back a stampede of buffalo plus fog and spot lights enough to light a small town. 'You follow dig?' said the brothers.

'At least fifty yards, git it?'

'Right,' sniffled Leroy thoroughly cowered.

Chapter 11

That same morning, the Works Manager C J Fishbone, who had a large wart at the centre of his forehead and with half his mind on his upcoming letting go by the new owners, his firing in fact, which pleased the owners no end; no redundancy money to pay out and it was all because of his ineptitude in dealing with the lopping off of Coley's ear. They cunningly gave him a month's grace to avoid any employment issues. 'No, no, not firing,' said the owners when he bitterly complained, 'consider it a case of involuntary redundancy, a matter of deconstruction.' He now came whining to Sheriff Guber that gear and stuff were going missing from the works in the blind and but hopeless faith of regaining favour with the new owners and management.

'It must have been a small army to take all that stuff you say in a such short time. The County hasn't an army of any sort. Must have bin Mainlanders. Not my jurisdiction, not my domain.' Guber paused for breath; he knew intuitively that the manager was overstating his case. Probably here to cover his ass. 'There are no scrap metal merchants here either in any case.'

'Plenty of bullshit merchants, though,' said the manager under his breath, 'and you are one of them.' He laughed inwardly.

'Though ya need to look over the Mainland,' continued the Sheriff who heard every word but didn't bat an eyelash. 'Git your insurers on to it, that's the best thing, help I can't, so I shan't. Bye.' He wrote on a report then began plucking the hairs out of his nose while pretending to read a file in front of him. The bemused manager left shaking his head but it all went much as he expected and he was on record as having notified the authorities at least such as it was.

The Sheriff pondered for a moment. He had observed small trucks and vans taking away little parts of the Works for days. In the most likely scenario; some of the drivers were diverting the highly valued items to unscrupulous scrap dealers on the Mainland with the connivance of the manager. Why bother after the way they were sure to treat him after the peninsular sank? *Ah stuff it, all too complicated, wot he worry or give a flying gnat's ass? No siree.* There had been no armed robberies, murders, or assaults on the peninsular since his appointment; well, none that were reported anyway and there wasn't going to be any on his watch. There was the isolated case of the teenager who ran off from Jack's Crackerjack Burger and Chicken joint without paying. But he eventually paid though with a broken lip and tooth as well as a badly bruised hip from a flying kick from the Sheriff when he was found and cornered.

'I'll kill ya an ya mongrel family if you complain, understand!' The beaten boy could only nod and crawl painfully away.

'Tell all ya girlie friends bout this as a warning, go do ya shit on the Mainland not here!' The Sheriff lay back in his chair gloating about his exploits and daydreamed about being famous anonymously.

Chapter 12

With the morning fog dissipating, Serena walked back to the Advocate and threw her sandwich in a rubbish bin on the way. On passing the Sheriff's Office, she brushed by a man coming out with a wart on his forehead and a smile on his face. *At least someone was happy,* she thought and continued on to the Advocate. Safely inside she remarked to Sidney Stilton, 'What's with all the horse faces out there?' *Here too,* she thought.

'The Works is off to the Mainland, the workers who won't follow are to be let go, redundancies galore,' replied Sidney.

A worker standing nearby, a woman with a forehead wart and a witch's nose and a sombre voice said, 'Most don't want to move because they say the Mainlanders look down their noses at them, call our county The Pen, the pricks. Prejudice. Most want to blow up the bridge to the Mainland. It's down the gurgler or the pisshole eef you prefer. For workers, shops and us and all ever.'

Sidney added, ''Cept for those two big 'orrible bozos who won large at Lotto and couldn't care less anyway,' he said enviously.

The word was out via Bald Maude who never kept her trap shut as a matter of principle. 'I'm only telling the truth aint I; I aint gossiping, aint I ever.'

Feeling low and bored, Serena wandered out of the office again and sidestepped into the Thistle Inn pub. It took a moment to adjust to the dingy surroundings and the flickering light. The bar rooms reeked of stale beer and cigarette smoke, the carpet once red was bare in patches and discoloured in others by multi-coloured squelching mixtures of what she didn't want to know but by now she desperately needed a drink. Holding her breath, she advanced upon the bar and ordered a large gin and tonic from Solemn Sam who raised his one and only eyebrow quizzically at the newcomer. Serena retired to the booth closest to the doors at least to get some fresh air and to feel safer if she had to make a run for it.

In the confines of the booth, her stomach settled. *No ice, blast*, she thought taking a sip of her drink. No one appeared interested in the sports programme bubbling and blurting off key from the TV over the long bar.

Everything was discordant. She put on a pair of sunglasses, strangely the lights became clearer and the surroundings more defined, to her city eyes the place seemed half full of mumbling heavily bearded trolls and assorted red-necked good old boys, most wearing a mishmash of camouflage gear and caps worn every which way but straight; they appeared like the surviving remnants from some bygone rebel guerrilla group.

Well, I'm incognito, I'm here but not here, she wanly smiled: from iced cocktails in Manhattan, rubbing shoulders with the rich, the famous and the self-ordained fabulous; to warm gin, writing death columns and trying to avoid the inhabitants of *The Twilight Zone.*

In vivid contrast, an attractive woman sat cross-legged on one of the bar stools. Oddly, none of the men in the bar paid her any attention except a skinny guy. The woman was preening herself, she was dressed in a white miniskirt tight over her haunches, a clinging pink sweater, make-up enough for two women, Frisbee-sized gold hoop earrings; her crowning glory was a wild, disordered thing of deepest black.

Quite suddenly, Serena's view was blocked. Standing in front of her was a very pretty woman with large breasts wearing a tight-fitting sheaf of a dress. She had an enormous head of curly blonde hair. 'Beat it,' she said in a rasping smoker's voice, 'my patch,' she said with her hands on her ample hips.

Serena summed up the situation at once and taking off her sunglasses said, 'I'm just in for a quick drink. Sorry, I didn't know this was your place, please forgive me.' Good grief, a Dolly Parton lookalike!

The blonde looked at Serena critically up and down and then relented. 'Ah, what the hell, sugar, I could do with some normal company, you are normal, aren't you? Normal's as rare as a herd of quagmires round here,' she squeezed herself into the other side of the booth. 'Names Hedy.'

'Sar-uh Serena, I'm as normal as one gets around here, I guess,' replied Serena ruefully putting on a friendly smile, 'I'm new here.'

'That I gathered, there's a bar not much better than here, next door if you prefer?'

'No, I'm comfortable for the moment.'

'Good,' replied Hedy, 'only the odd goofball and bald baboons back there anyway. What brings you to the end of the world ever?'

Serena thought for a moment. 'I'm a trainee newspaper reporter, a new career, starting at the bottom with the Advocate.'

'Well, you couldn't start much lower than that,' replied Hedy, thinking bullshit, but returning her smile.

They appraised each other doing a quick inventory; no make-up, rouge, genuine blonde, hardly any lipstick, lipstick past the lip line, nice suit, loose thread, full-blown breasts encapsulated in a too-tight bra, tad overweight, underfed, short pink nails, scarlet talons, Chanel, cigarette smoke, flash bag.

What's up? thought Hedy, *Hiding? Divorce imminent? On the lam. Gone to ground, but for what? Oh well, live and let live.*

Local beauty, still tip-toeing around her options, perhaps an ill mother or father – being a martyr conjectured Serena, far too many variables though, forget it. Be here in the moment, well in this particular moment she wished she was in the Caribbean or it's opposite the Switz Alps in winter she thought looking around the bar. The two began chatting. Sylvester brought Hedy an evil yellow concoction. 'Ta Sweet. Another for my new friend here whatever she's having with bloody ice this time.'

'Standing order,' Hedy explained the barman's service. 'Bet he would like to wear my dress, silly fat fart.'

'Isn't the women at the bar competition?'

'That's Gloria, hell no, she's an exhibitionist and a dominatrix, sadist as well as if that wasn't enough, the nearest we got to a pole dancer round here. Thinks she's hot as an Alabama asphalt road in high summer. More like frozen frost onna wire fence in Alaska ever,' she drawled then laughed, it was a surprisingly sweet laugh. Serena found herself liking her.

Hedy continued tossing her hair, 'Queer as a two-headed chipmunk, tried it on me once, no go, now she hates me. Get her rocks off having men ogle her. Most of the men in here rather be reamed out with barbed wire than have anything to do with her. However, she does have a small clientele who like that like type of thing, whips and such. It's whispered half the Town Council Members dig it. She gets a bigger and longer rectangular box in a plain brown wrapper in the mail every third month, but everything has its limits, stopped now, ha-ha, only joking,' she said looking at Serena's incredulous face.

They became aware of a tall, handsome man with broad shoulders standing over them. He was dark from working in the sun and he had even white teeth that shone as he smiled, it was a shy but nice smile. He held an old wide-brimmed straw hat with a faded red band in front of him with both delicate but work-hardened hands. He had his eyes cast down. His long dark eyelashes lay on his high sculptured cheekbones. *Well now surprise, an Adonis*, thought Serena, *a beauty among beasts.*

'Ooh ooh, cuse me, can-can I-I have a d-dance Miss Hedy mamma-m, ma?' he stuttered and stammered.

Serena blushed for him.

'Sure, Abner honey,' Hedy replied downing her drink with a flourish of her gold-bangled wrist. 'Nice to meet you, Serena, but duty calls, my favourite don't you know,' she said smiling and winking at Serena. *And no wonder,* thought Serena. Perhaps he's why she is still here. But she was not one to pry into other people's business, ha, that's a laugh that was her old job description in a nutshell. Serena returned her eyes to the women at the bar. Gloria untwined her long legs in front of the skinny man at the table with 'Council' embossed on the back of his overalls. The man was clearly entranced. He was plucking up Dutch courage; he had downed multiple Southern Comforts while she was watching him. His face was pink and his hands were trembling; Serena had a perfect view of this little drama. Gloria crossed her long legs again, unknown to Serena; she had been teasing him for weeks. The man started to get up on shaky knees. *Here we go,* thought Serena and wished Hedy was here to share this little moment of theatre.

The man wobbled up to Gloria. 'I think you are beautiful, I love y—' was as far as he got. Gloria slowly looked him up and down as if he was something nasty she had picked up on her shoe.

'Look buster, I poop and pees just like you sitting down ha; so get lost, go play with yourself ever,' she said in a braying voice so loud everyone could hear. The council worker shrunk in size and head down slunk to the toilets where to his shame, he carried out her order. Serena thought, *what an evil bitch,* she wanted out of here.

The Council worker whose name was Edward Elmwood aka Skinny Eddie steeled himself, got his act mostly together and strode back through the bar, haughtily ignoring what he thought was his true love, he went to the double doors to flash them open with a bit of manly pride, remembering too late they opened inward, squashed his face against the unyielding glass. 'Ha-ha.' He laughed hysterically. 'Always gets me.' He stumbled out onto the road and checked Main Street up and down for Sheriff Galoot Guber or Just-about; it seemed clear. 'Got work to do,' he said to himself, 'gotta erect signs atta Hope Beach and Charity Point.'

He made his way to his Council pick-up truck and checked the tray out; orange traffic cones, two bags of cement, shingle, a shovel and drum of water, a bucket and two white four-by-four poles with signs freshly painted with red letters. One which read, *STOP! Dumping of Rubbish of All kinds of this Point is Strictly Forbidden and in smaller letters: $200 fine by order of Council.* The other, *DANGER Subsidence, Keep Hard Right.*

'Shite for brains, Yankee pricks,' muttered Eddie, the most derogatory terms he could muster as he climbed unsteadily into the cab.

Chapter 13

Serena followed Skinny Eddie out the door very shortly afterwards. The fog had fully dissipated thank goodness. Flash of light again at the top of the hill. Back to the office, slap bang into Lowell. 'Ah, Miss ah…'

'Call me Serena,' said Serena magnanimously, the gin kicking in. 'What's up on the hill?' she enquired.

She's talking to me, thought Lowell with relief. 'The Castle,' he answered pulling on his long earlobes.

'Castle?' she queried.

'Well, probably not a real one, a mad American Scotchman's idea of one. One of the original Hooks who own it struck it big in the Yukon or the Klondike ever, found a gold nugget as big as a boot, banked half of it and invested in oil or some new-fangled thing back then with the other half ever. Owns most of the Peninsular some say.'

Serena looked at him sceptically. 'Who lives up there now?' she enquired.

'Last of the line, Captain Hook, mad as a skinned snake, rumoured he keeps slaves but I would discount that, probably servants doesn't mix with us lowlanders. I don't think he likes us.'

That's in his favour thought Serena. 'Gives interviews does he?' asked Serena her journalistic instincts aroused.

'Not likely, but you could try, hum, maybe there's a story in it, got to go, go for it, bye um, Serena. Just proofread the public notices, ads and write up the deaths columns before you pursue your assignment er…story each day. Take all the time you need.'

Mr Lowell, smiled to himself, a sign from above with her mostly out of his sight he was less likely to have his neck broken and he wasn't paying her a nickel. A win-win situation for him. Of course, any reportage of hers wouldn't hold a candle to the Crab Thing. That was a miracle five years ago. What a boon, what a seller, even his big paper hard-ass cousin was impressed and had it syndicated far and wide.

The first-hand storey from the protagonists, a couple from the Mainland with their baby Jonah decided to camp the evening under canvas on Hope Beach so they zigzagged down off the side road from the road leading to Charity Point and onto the beach above the high tide mark the early evening. The hurricane lamp hanging on the centre pole was lit low and all was very cosy, the weather balmy, a lazy sea rumbled softly sixty yards away. Joe had young Jonah nestled on his side of the tent and Jeanette spooning into him on the right. Stars twinkled through the flap in the tent. There was a faded moon. Joe had reached up and turned off the lamp with a twist. Serenity; sweet calm reined.

The rumble when it came was a shock, it felt as if half the beach had slid into the sea; which wasn't quite true. A huge undersea shelf had collapsed into the depths disturbing the many denizens living there. Now they were on the move, hundreds of them, crawling, scuttling sideways, shuffling, sensing and doing what giant inshore crabs do, their glowing stalked eyes open for new opportunities and above all, food.

They marched as an army up the beach towards the tent and car. The campers first inkling the horde was upon them was the tearing and renting of the fabric of the tent by claws, nippers and other crusty appendages that reached in and clutched Jonah from Joe's despairing hands. He and his wife screaming tried to dislodge the giant crabs but they, in turn, turned on them both, nipping and biting with scalding effects, they were being skinned alive.

'Run for the car while we still can!' Joe had screamed. They careened towards the car thrusting off the clutching demons, got in and turned the headlights on, and saw the horrible sight of their poor Jonah being carried back into the sea. The lights appeared to have frightened the crabs and en mass they had retreated. In shock and hysterical, the couple had dialled 111. Editor Lowell reflected back on this exclusive news with wonderment and fond memories.

Chapter 14

On the hill, the bell trilled three times. Damn. Oh well, give his brain a workout. The Captain finished his wine bottle and put it to one side, Millie took away the debris of his breakfast. He lay back in his chair; this was peaceful except there was someone coming to ruin it for him. An old battered brown Buick was making its way up between the elms. 'Blast!' he exclaimed, he would have to take down his father's lawyers shingle from the front gate sometime if he ever remembered. People thought that his father's lawyer's degree was hereditary or something. He didn't mind too much, it gave him some interest. Most clients never returned and the Captain suspected it was just curiosity in the first place that made them come. Of course, he never went near a court room and he gave only advice on trivial things that had become knotted in the heads of the complainants. However, at the moment, he could have done without a visitor or a client. The car stopped under the portico; a squat man with a pug nose squeezed himself out.

'Afternoon, Captain Hook, a fair day.'

'What brings you here, Mr Scmelling?'

'I run the shoe shop in town,' he said proudly. Perhaps he could sell the Captain some shoes. He looked around him in awe. *Not a chance probably gets his directly from Italy*, he thought disappointed.

'I'm aware of your profession, Mr Scmelling,' said the Captain shaking Scmelling's left hand, 'please sit down.' The Captain proffered a chair.

'Thank you, won't keep you long, Captain, it's me, neighbour, you see,' he said sitting down and giving a sidewise glance at the Captain hook.

'I surely hope so. Your neighbour you say?'

'Yeah, every damn Saturday and Sunday mornin', early, he starts up his lawnmower, bloody weed-eater, hedge trimmers, chainsaw.' He paused for breath. 'His water-blaster. I swear, Captain, I could kill him, I've a mind to shove his water-blaster up his nether regions and turn it on full blast.'

'Hum, I think even own esteemed Sheriff Guber would have something to say about that,' he said with irony.

'That ficcing galoot,' scoffed Mr Scmelling going all pink in the face. 'Excuse me language, sir.'

'Have you spoken to your neighbour about his thoughtlessness?'

'We don't talk, he's up himself. Him and his new hybrid car and snooty wife.'

'Have you tried earmuffs?'

'What, in bed,' It was affecting his love life as well, such as it was.

'Earplugs?'

There was a sullen silence. The Captain knew he was not on his best game.

'Wait here, Mr Scmelling.' The captain shot away to his liquor cabinet, pulled out a whiskey bottle, opened it and grabbed a couple of shot glasses and returned. 'Drink this, it relieves most anxiety they say. Start up your own machines very early on Friday mornings; your neighbour will get the point,' he concluded hoping the neighbour wasn't violent and had a gun. A few more drinks. The Captain had a couple of large ones, not bad after all; after a number that is, went down as smooth as hot ice now, have a few more. They talked about the weather, the Indian summer, hurricanes, cyclones, tornadoes and so forth. Scmelling drank his whisky beginning with a grimace that turned to a grin after a three or was it four? *What! Bottle half empty, Good Lord*, thought the Captain. He passed the rest of the bottle over as a gift to Mr Scmelling. Giving away twenty-three-year-old single malt Scotch, he must be a loony: he bet that Scmelling couldn't even tell the difference between it and a rude rudimentary one-year-old.

'Thanks, Captain, bless you, bless you, bye-bye now, bye,' blathered Scmelling, staggering to his feet. 'Bye.'

'Bye,' returned the Captain in relief slumping back down in his seat that suddenly felt like an air cushion. He mopped his brow with his silk handkerchief. 'Whew.' A naked flame near him and he was likely to explode from the whiskey fumes. He pictured himself jetting flame from all his orifices and shooting up and about like some party balloon. Then a germ of an idea flashed through his mind and lodged in an unpolluted brain cell. He watched with one eye the old Buick farting and burping spasmodically as it left and threaded its unsteady way down through the elms to the gatehouse a quarter mile away. Easy fodder for the gruesome Sheriff Guber, the Captain realised belatedly.

Manhandle let Scmelling through the gate with a shake of his head.

Chapter 15

Later in the day, the Captain recovered, watched a helicopter thump over the Castle grounds then settle itself on his golf course at the rear of the Castle. In it were his and his staff's fortnightly food, provisions and such. The three Ms, Manhandle, Marie and Millie would sort it out and store it including the bottled water and whatever else that needed to be done. Shortly after, the dragonfly groped its way upwards, banked then it was swiftly away over the sea its blades flashing in the sun back to the Mainland. The Captain had a standing order with the owners of the craft. Among his other contacts were his bank manager with his ingratiating voice, his cheerful accountant, an astute lawyer and a property manager and other lesser but necessary people to look after his interests and comfort. He used his landline when he needed them, he liked the phone's simplicity. He had tried a cell phone but once, but with his artificial hand he could not manipulate the buttons and other gadgets and in a fit of uncommon rage threw it to the ground and stomped on it and that was the end of another piece of techno-junk as he called such stuff as far as he was concerned.

Chapter 16

Tic and Tac arrived at the pub and then as arranged Leroy, who snuck into the bar on his bandy legs.

'What's big deal then ever?' enquired Tic and Tac after drinks were gathered.

'Got the lot, speed, ecstasy, other crazy shit, knock out pills that act quick smart and knock the gals right out of their pants ha-ha, especially for you.'

'Well, would you know it? Just what we ordered for the shit list.'

'Hey what?' asked Leroy mystified.

'No busyness of yours.' Leroy didn't know it, but a quick phone call had been made to Ugly Auntie from the pub moments before, verifying the price and the merchandise. 'Right, check,' was the brusque reply, then silence.

'Got's lots. Maybe dear but the real deal. Never done no one wrong, now have I?' That was true, besides no one crossed Ugly Auntie and lived above water.

Leroy passed over a shopping bag, both Tic and Tac quickly looked through the bag, then it disappeared into Tac's copious jacket. Cash changed hands under the table; three rounds of drink sealed the deal.

'Blow now, ice hole,' they said dismissively.

He gladly got up and left, it had taken all his courage just to sit with them. He passed an old man hunched in the corner as he went. *How could the man bear to even sit in the same room with them,* he wondered.

Chapter 17

'25 to 45.'

'Yeah, Just-about,' replied the Sheriff.

'Got you a real live one, should be arrested for his hair alone. Purple Charger, headin' out of town.'

'I'm up and away ten four,' Oh sweet joy. He wheeled his police car around to block off the bridge to the mainland.

Leroy, half pissed but alert in this crazy town, spotted Guber's car ahead and did a hasty U-turn and headed back inland to hide up or circle back when the heat grew tired. But no, lights started flashing the siren wailed, and the pig was onto him. He blasted back down the main road, and passed a man with three hands or was he holding gloves? Ah, countryside now, surely he could outdistance the swine behind not realising he was running out of distance and Guber's car had been supercharged for just this sort of eventuality. Leroy dragged deeply on a joint for relief.

At the same time, well ahead, Skinny Eddie drove to the entry of Hope Beach and erected the subsidence sign then the short distance up to Charity Point where he dug another hole placed in the other warning sign and cemented it in; laid traffic cones on the edge of the subsidence then backed his truck into some scrub for concealment and took a big glug from a jug of White Lighting he had bought from a itinerate moonshiner for emergencies. With anguish eroding his guts, he relived his humiliation at the pub.

Back down the road, Guber was closing in on his man till finally, he pulled him over. He walked slowly and purposely back to the purple Charger, pulling down his shades. Leroy's head and hair was hanging out the side window and he was desperately trying to puff out the last drag of the hash in his lungs but only succeeded in blowing it up the Sheriff's honker. Guber suddenly felt woozy but he was able to grab Leroy's hair. Leroy instinctively reacted and quickly wound the window up and accelerated off with his face stuck to the window and with most of his heavy hair outside blowing dirty yellow in the slipstream. Blast, he couldn't free his hair, wind down the window and drive properly all at the same time, so squished sideways he erratically carried on. 'Come back you cityite heathen!' yelled Gruder running swiftly back to his car and getting in the wrong side wondering who the hell had stolen his steering wheel, then clarity, quickly changing seats and pulling out in hot pursuit heading for Charity Point, with his siren screaming and gun out waving it through the window all the while bellowing like a banshee.

Leroy saw they were now following a long coastline, surely the road cut across and connected back to the top of this island of the damned and escape? *Not the road to nowhere surely, not a dead end,* he thought in panic. He finally pulled his hair free and the wound turned down the side window. In his side vision mirror, he didn't like the sight of the large black bore of Guber's .44 at all. He stretched into his glove compartment for some sort of weapon or even a white flag, shit nothing; a Mars Bar and a Stars and Stripes condom was all, he threw them out the window in despair. He registered the subsidence sign ahead and the orange cones but briefly, kept on, the hole in the side of the road tore off his left rear tyre, the muffler and brakes lines but momentum carried him on and with a terrible screech and scream from both car and occupant fell over the sixty foot drop off Charity Point and into the sea. The crusty-limbed denizens below stirred. Guber avoiding the subsidence skidded to a smoky halt just short of the drop and got out and leaning on the new sign yelled down, 'Good riddance to bad rubbish!' The sign, the cement still wet, collapsed over the cliff taking the astonished, unbelieving Sheriff with it.

Part 2

Chapter 1

Skinny Eddie hiding in his truck at the point saw it all but lashed up from the drink and risked the sack; he couldn't and wouldn't abide that. He couldn't report it, not in his state. He was at a loss. *What to do?* he thought scratching at his balding head. Then it came to him, he would push the Sheriff's car over Charity Point as well; it would look like a high-speed chase gone horribly wrong. It started to rain; he ignored it and walked down to the car, opened the driver's door and released the handbrake. The car rolled forward and disappeared almost silently through the misty rain. Then wet and cold, lit off home to sleep and sober up; thankfully it was the end of yet another long and miserable day for him.

Crafty Chester Crawford, a crab fisherman, one of only three on the Peninsular, was fishing below and around from the point heard all commotion above but ignored it. None of his business was as he saw it besides he was busy; the weight gauge on his derrick hanging over the bluff around the corner showed the crab cage was full to the brim. He smiled to himself, *what a catch*. He started the old motor and started quickly reeling up the easy unloading topless cage. The smaller top crabs usually fell out first, followed by the main catch then the rotten bait fish and meat if any remained. This time it was different; the unintentional bait fell out first; a grisly head, fleshless except for a single eye looking at him quizzically. A body or all that remained of one in a torn and tattered blue uniform, its hands, most of the feet and even its shoes had been partly eaten. A gun and a Sheriff's Star remained intact. *Oh, God-damn, brain complications*, a condition he loathed, not since Viet Nam had he seen anything like it. Must be what all the noise was about earlier. He slumped his head in his arms, *what to do? Think*, he commandeered himself. First things first, he decided. He put on his yellow sou-wester against the rain and sudden cold and made his way up to Charity Point. The obvious was there to see. He had heard the high-speed chase, the siren, and gave a cursory look round, he saw the double skid marks, the scattered road cones and car litter on the road and came to the only conclusion that made sense. 'Well, I'll be, the dern ding-dong dings.' He grinned out of his crumpled face.

But there was more than this to contemplate; his business for instance. Five years ago, his crab enterprise was all but ruined by a Mainlanders kid being eaten alive. Almost put him out of business after people became squeamish about eating crab meat. It didn't help the County area's economy either for the Peninsular was known for its crab, all much to the dismay of the Mayor. But even the most horrible of events are either forgotten or fade, just hanging on and surviving was what really mattered. Crafty got a job at the Works till memories lapsed. He went back to the derrick and his shack whereby he threw overboard the remains of Gruder. Seagulls squawked, cawed and wheeled overhead. Crafty went inside out of the rain, lit his potbelly stove and put on a tin of beef stew. *Heard nothing, saw nothing, did nothing guys,* he rehearsed to himself.

Chapter 2

Deputy Just-about Early was slightly bothered. Not a word from Guber since his last call. He had radioed 45 a number of times to no avail; perhaps he should follow up and go looking? He went to his car and drove to the bridge, his last contact. Nothing. He headed out to Charity Point at the opposite end of the Peninsula. The rain had stopped. At that point, he found the skid marks and so forth that didn't take a great brain to work out but the big mystery was the Mars Bar, *what the hell was it doing there? Was someone trying to confuse the evidence?* With his mind adrift he drove slowly back to the station. He would call the Mayor and the Sheriff's Office on the Mainland. He had no regrets for Guber; he had enough of his up-up and aways. He would go home, watch TV and cover up under a blanket on his couch for protection against the crap which was sure to fly about any time soon. When at home for comfort food he ate the Mars Bar.

Chapter 3

Serena was relatively happy for the first time in a while, she had an assignment. Perhaps even better than what she was used to; recording the goings on of the rich, the famous and the self-ordained celebrities' in her old domain, their mindless happenings, who was in rehab who had come out, who was up who was down, who was in who and the like. Now, this Captain Hook could prove interesting. Maybe her future beckoned up on the hill, perhaps a possible escape from purgatory, a serious moneyed eccentric was going to get a visit whether he liked it or not.

The object of Serena's attention, Captain Hook was well mellowed on his afternoon wine, but his mind was busy nevertheless. *1708, 1708, what was the terrible disaster?* He sorted through the many papers he had accumulated and came across an old diary, the name inside the cover was indecipherable but the content turned out to be gold briefly explaining everything. He began reading the archaic writing interpreting as he read; he skimmed till he came across:

"*25 November 1708:*

God, we are forsaken. Calamity, the devil has shaken the ground and cut off your bountiful peninsular from the mainland in the night, thirty souls are winging their way to you, forgive them their trespasses, my dear Lord…"

25th November that's Celebration Day in the County, what kind of county celebrated a disaster, he questioned himself. A jackass one that's for sure. Manhandles buzzer trilled three times breaking into his thoughts. Peter, Paul and Mary, just when he was getting somewhere. Better get another bottle of wine.

Serena drove the beaten-up Ford slowly up the long drive that led to the imposing Castle. She saw a tall man get up from a lounger outside the portico and go inside and come out again with a bottle, cooler and glasses and arrange another lounger around the glass-topped table. *At least he looks normal,* thought Serena watching, which was more than she could say for the car as it shuddered to a stop.

'Sorry for the company car, such as it is,' apologised Serena getting out the squealing door and approaching the man, ready in her handbag was her notebook and pen; she had forgone electronic recording devices for a while.

'No need, Ma'am, Captain Hook,' he replied introducing himself and giving a slight bow. *About twenty, twenty-two,* he thought.

'Serena Pussyfoot,' putting out her right hand and seeing the hook quickly changed hands. He took it and shook it firmly with no fuss. If he was one-card-short-of-a-full-deck it wasn't obvious thought Serena, *not bad looking either,* Brad Pitt came to mind. She was delighted by the shiny steel hook for a hand, shades of Peter Pan and Co.

'What can I do for you?' He said taking in her stylish clothing, shoes and handbag. *A red-haired beauty. Obviously not from hereabouts. Good Lord, the bouncing apparition in the telescope!* He offered her a cool chardonnay, and then politely asked her why she was there.

'That would be nice,' she replied cordially took the proffered seat and sat down.

'A fine wine,' she said after taking a sip.

'Thank you.'

'Could you have Marie get us a platter, Michael?' requested the Captain of Manhandle who had magically appeared on his right elbow.

'Back to my original question,' he softly inquired when Manhandle had departed.

'I'm a journalist, from the local paper, getting a little local colour.'

Why was she slumming at that rag? Some sort of obligation she was fulfilling? he thought.

She said, 'A small obligation to fulfil,' as if reading his mind. They smiled at each other. Instant rapport. *Well-well,* they thought simultaneously.

Marie arrived shortly back with the platter. 'Thanks kindly, Marie,' said the Captain and introduced Serena.

'Afghanistan,' said the captain after Marie had left, tapping his hook as if no other explanation was called for and it didn't. He poured each of them another wine and they helped themselves to the antipasto.

'Did you know that Peninsular County was actually a self-supporting peninsular before it became an island with a connecting bridge to the Mainland as you see now? No. Well, it became a large island after a violent earthquake in 1708, but they still call it a Peninsular,' he said, imparting his recent knowledge and preparing to embellish as he went along.

'There's a real maelstrom of troubled waters under the bridge, even now,' replied Serena.

'It's where two very strong coastal currents meet, north against south, just like the war. They say when the two parts separated, a settlement of thirty people were swept away, and boulders as big as houses and cars were hurled against each. The Peninsular shook like jelly; the north end of this edifice behind us collapsed, killing two chambermaids and a guest, most of the town was destroyed, and the old building you work in miraculously survived.' Boy was this wine working or not? Besides, he wasn't about to let reality get in the way of a good story, was he?

'I was working for a prodigious paper in New York and I wrote an article on these people, thought they were celebrities you know, too close to the bone, got lazy, should have researched more, turned out they were gangsters. Drug barons and bloody murderers. Had to flee for my very life. Hence my being here till things cool down,' she spouted with self-disgust in her voice. 'But, there they were, hobnobbing with the rich and the famous,' she added indignantly.

'Yes, I can believe that.' Not believing a word of it, but should he care? The beautiful apparition was sitting right across the table from him.

He continued, 'Now here because the original inhabitants couldn't reach the Mainland they inbred for nearly seventy years. Originally, they were a religious sect, and as outcasts, they trekked here to avoid persecution or more likely, prosecution. Probably practised incest or something like it ever. No wonder the population is inbred.' The Captain didn't know it, but it wasn't far from the truth, which was in short supply on both sides of the table. 'You may have seen the odd throwback or three in town.'

'Sure have.' It all made sense in a peculiar way even if most of Hook's story was pure hokum. Thank heavens it wasn't something in the water. With apprehension, she had had the odd glass or two and had showered in it. *No bottled water in the town; how primitive can you get?* She thought.

'More wine?' he asked admiring her crossed legs.

'Yes please,' she was happy and flattered by the attention. 'I can't keep calling you, Captain, what's your real name if you don't mind that is?'

'Richard Hook, Rick, "*Of all the bars in the world, you just happen to walk into mine,*"' he mimicked.

'Casablanca! One of my favourite films. Humphrey Bogart, Bergman. Rates as a classic alongside Gone with the Wind. Clark Gable, "*Frankly my dear, I couldn't give a damn.*"' They both laughed in delight.

They continued to make small talk. Serena said, 'The Crest and motto over the gate "Fortuna Juvat," sorry my Latin is not up to scratch.'

'Most people down there think it's French Canadian, from the Yukon perhaps or somewhere where the family fortune was first made. The Crest is a stylised Scotch Thistle, Scotland's national flower; the motto means "Fortune Favours the Brave."'

'Do you believe that?'

'Most of the brave I've known have ended up mostly dead,' he replied with sad cynicism. 'Beware going home, monsters abound,' continued Rick looking at the slipping sun.

'Yes, I know, I've seen some.'

'Probably not this one, I'll get Manhandle to run you home and pick you up and bring you back in the morning for the car. We have an overzealous Sheriff who gets his kicks apprehending drinking drivers,' he said in explanation.

'Coffee?'

'Black please.'

'Right oh, my poison also.' He called Marie and made the arrangements. When the coffee arrived, he looked into Serena's green eyes as he vibrated the sugar in his cup with his hook to her surprise and amusement then saw her off. They both promised to see each other the next day at about eleven for brunch. Manhandle drove Serena off in the family limo, she looked down at her bag and notebook in surprise, she hadn't written a thing. They had left each other satisfied. *A date,* they both thought simultaneously. The Captain eventually went to bed happier than he had been for a long time under the peaceful glow of the lowering sun. In Serena, the problem of the history editing, etc., had an obvious solution. In all, it had been a nice day mostly round. Manhandle who had overseen things behind the scenes, smiled to himself; he would see Marie, of whom he was very fond of, as he was loyal to the good Captain later.

Chapter 4

'We'll funnel 'em towards the new water trough come punch bowl and cups,' drawled Tic.

'Big glasses and a dipper,' interjected Tac.

'Yeah, ever. Big sign, somethin' like, "Get it while it lasts – punch with a real punch."'

'Cool. A truckload of lemonade, an iceberg of ice. Keg of coke, huge saucepans of vodka, buckets of gin, wheelbarrows of bourbon, cut a lemonade tree down for slices of lemon on top fancy like, leave the leftover booze scattered about.'

'Then flashing lights, streamers. Speed and all that other sissy shit is thrown into the punch for the dancers and singers, knock-out pills for those on the list.'

'At the centre of the table, paper towels, plastic plates, chunks of crab, plenty of chicken and ham and other stuff, darn, hey starting to get lockjaw from all's this thinking and jabbering,' complained Tac, 'Pass the jug, would you?'

'Music, good old Pa's fifty-sixty stuff, mostly party Rock! Bill Haley, Elvis, Fats Domino.' They badly mimed Fats playing the piano and sang in surprisingly rich baritones, the words probably incorrect but it did not matter a jot, the tone was the thing:

...Well I'm walking to New Orleans
Ma honey spent all ma money
Got no money for the rent
Ma money is all been spent
So I'm walking to New Orleans...

They were weird beings with a strange talent for singing.

'And new stuff by Hogtie and the Bagpipes.'

'The Blowfish.'

'Ever.'

'Clubs for the over violent. Music, Roy Orbison, Johnny Cash, Jerry Lee, maybe Dolly Parton, not our local Hedy, flashing her boo boo her ooh ooh – tits. Oh and we better sweep the floor,' Tac added.

'And maybe we dress up as surgeons, in white masks, caps and our white boots as well, how about that?' yelled Tic with self-amazement.

'Yeah yeah, Gawd, I don't know where we get them ideas, we must be ficcing genies.'

'Out the back, the real stuff, hooks, power saws, a bin for cast-off bits, pliers and probes laid out on a table to set the scene, huh.'

'Gotta order a Porta-loo, can't have donkeys coming out back to use ours and seein' what we are really up to.'

'Can't wait, for all this,' said Tac, the top of his head and what could be seen of his face was a bright red all aglow like the previous night's sunset... 'Still the problem of the invites, date, times and other mutt and stuff.'

'Off to the pub then, for a brain hurricane?'

'Well dill my pickle, me thought exactly, say no more, I'm burning up with good stuff and me guts needs fixin' like General Lee's after Gettysburg.'

***

In the back bar of the pub sat Haldenstein, his eyes cold and calculating, the pain under his ribs agonising but he endured. *Ah, here are my boys as usual.* He started filling out a greeting card in his delicate handwriting after all he had been a Master Forger in another life and still had his contacts as well. A completed card lay open on the table in full view as bait for the boys as they came in. Tic and Tac entered and ordered their drinks and shuffled past glancing at him and his table. Haldenstein's ostentation prepared another card.

'Did you see that? Clever old bugger.' The brothers could barely write at all.

'Does no harm.'

'Yeah, but them cards. Professional like. Know what I'm thinking?'

'As always, I'm onto ya, impress all the suckers.'

'For money, I bet he would.'

'Ask him over. We got some suading to do. Oh, your round, getta phone book as well.'

'What for?'

'For names and addresses, numbnuts.' Tac moved away not the least bit offended. He would get pen and paper as well to show just how brainy he truly was.

Chapter 5

Captain Hook awoke fully refreshed for the new day his brain was fully firing all fuses and circuit breakers intact. He got out of bed his brain abuzz, nine o'clock, was the right time for climbing into new ideas. He rang his solicitor then his accountant, bank and property manager, and one after another, they were all positive about his proposed casino plan etc. He would pass his ideas in front of Serena when she arrived and perhaps he could slip in the matter of the peninsular history. He spoke to Marie and Millie about having breakfast upon the battlements; it was a day of no wind and a warming sun. *A day full of possibilities ripe and juicy ready for picking,* he thought.

He rang Manhandle to pick Serena up as a VIP, then showered, shaved and carefully got dressed.

Serena likewise attentively groomed herself. She ensured the chewing gum was still blocking the peephole. The new day felt warm and full of hope. Even old Bald Maude walking to the Lotto shop below stark naked except for her old-fashioned dun-coloured no-frills underwear carrying her bag of Lotto overalls and shoes, left her unfazed. She watched as Bald Maude passed Chief Bluebluff's horse High Kick tied up outside the pub alongside a broken apart bale of hay and a wooden pail of water who looked at Maude with studied indifference but made a snort through its darkened purpled nostrils in recognition.

When Serena arrived at the castle, she was escorted by Manhandle up to the battlements, on the oak-panelled walls of the stairs hung battle scenes and portraits, stern men, all soldiers with the exception of an Admiral or something. They appeared to date from the American Revolution, the Civil War, the Indian and Mexican wars, World War One and Two and Korea. Below Serena was a vast reception hall, big enough for two basketball courts. Upstairs were a multitude of large rooms with their doors open, airing she presumed, led off left and right along the other wings of the Castle from the imposing curved staircase in its centre. Going higher still in the court area within the battlements there was white filigree furniture, the table dressed with a starched tablecloth and napkins as well as fine china and silverware. Under a clear warming cover there was an English breakfast, outside of the cover there was a pitcher of freshly iced orange juice, crystal flutes and a chilled bottle of champagne in a silver monogrammed ice bucket. A silver call bell sat apart at the corner of the table.

'Good morning.'

'Indeed, Rick, indeed.' She was astonished at the vastness of the view beyond, which was not apparent from the ground. Without thinking, he brought forward the telescope.

'Look through this.' She was slightly disconcerted – the source of the flashing light from the hill? She looked through it.

'Wow!' she exclaimed. She took a quick look at the newspaper office and its large bell tower. *Well, well,* she thought, *the bat from the belfry.* She could see Editor Lowell as clear as day outside the entry pulling down the clutch of his pants in the heat and mopping his brow as he went down the footpath in the general direction of the pub. They returned to the table. 'This is very civilised,' said Serena sitting down in her smart Prussian blue suit.

'Thank you,' replied the Captain.

Dressed chic as if for an interview, nice, he thought pouring each of them champagne. 'Cheers.' The sun was reaching for its height and it was becoming warm early. In the shade of a green and white striped canvas awning over the table, they started eating. 'Yes, not a bad view at all considering it's mostly ranch land,' said the Captain, smiling at her earlier remark.

'This food is really nice,' she said in appreciation taking in his Harris's tweed trousers, starched white shirt and dark brogue shoes.

'I bring it in from the Mainland. The local products are as good, if not better, the service and delivery, however, is abysmal and the hygiene suspect.'

'So, this is what Southern Hospitality is really like?' She smiled.

'An allusion. Enjoy it while it lasts. Not likely to continue, unfortunately,' he said exaggerating a little with a concerned look as he started his spiel.

'Why is that?'

'A Conglomerate, a Big Con, has drastic ideas for this County.' The Captain detested consortiums and large corporations of any kind as had his father and the fathers before him, all extolling their sins, their lack of accountability – they had neither honour nor loyalty; it was all smoke and mirrors, secret passageways, hidden trapdoors and rabbit burrows, not like the Army though he hated to say it. When the shit hit the fan, the top echelon became moles and went deep underground. He'd love to give this lot a real bloody nose and a black eye. However, he had to be mindful not to overdo things with Serena as he had often done in the past with other projects thereby sabotaging his own efforts by drink-induced uncontrolled blathering.

'They are of the opinion that we produce top quality prime beef but our methods are all wrong. Their plan briefly is to move production to the Mainland and pack and distribute from there.' He knew they secretly wanted to turn the whole peninsular including the Works and the town into extra pasture land leaving him and his castle marooned, but he wouldn't be hassled into fully mobilising his forces against this idea immediately. At the present moment, he was working on his paper sorting and editing agenda, which ran concurrently with the former.

He continued, 'Already starting to close the Meat Works. Going to set up the new one about ten miles in on the Mainland with its own shopping centre, mostly a new town to be named Faith. Incidentally, a further twenty miles away is Travis City, the nearest city north of here.'

'It all sounds typical to me,' said Serena.

The Captain grimaced. The vice of avarice in action was how he saw it.

'It is. Let me show you the County in detail from up here, that is if you have a mind to, bring your glass, I'll carry the bottle.'

Marie and Millie started clearing the table. Marie was especially cheerful. That was Manhandle's doing appraised Rick. Leaning over the battlements, Rick pointed out the meat works, market gardens and closer, his golf course below, strips and bunches of houses and shops further out with their weird architecture mostly made from the ruins of the Castles lost wing after the 1708 earthquake as he surmised.

'It's almost picturesque,' thought Serena, well from up here anyway pity about the inhabitants down there.

Hook owned most of the countryside but like most things nothing was unassailable. He didn't own the Works itself or a bit of bog land, the former hadn't mattered in the past, Hook had been the Chairman of the Works Board of Directors since forever. He, himself had not been invited onto the board, *it was an obvious slight and not an oversight as they probably dumbly hoped,* he thought. Hook had always been on the Board. He suspected a more likely motive; he conjectured that the Board had been bought off, besides he considered the Board and the Management a dim greedy lot anyway. With him on the Board, things could have been a lot different. He might have stuck only for a Works upgrade and stuff for instance. The Hook name would have carried a lot of weight in any event.

Hook with a grandiose sweep of his arms and hands indicated the vast expanse of ranch land stretching to the eastern horizon where only just could be seen some ranch buildings beside a large lake. He paused for breath and another drink.

'I have three full-time hands on the ranch under Randy the manager. It's all hands-off for me. In fact, I own most of the land you can see including the market gardens, all 'cept the Meat Works and a bit of bog,' he said all this in a modest tone. Serena was suitably impressed. The property was vast.

'So you see they are trying to outmanoeuvre me, although there is not much chance of that.' He took another drink and refilled her glass.

'Back to the Big Con, they are really only interested in the quality beef I produce here, neither the town nor its workers. The Peninsular climate and the soil are perfect for fat-feeding grass.'

'So the township would turn in all probability into a ghost town,' said Serena who had heard something similar at the Advocate recently.

She's intuitive, he thought thankfully. With some regret, he realised his family had done little for the township since the 1708 earthquake. Perhaps he could change that. There was the large concrete bridge connecting the Peninsular for sure, but that was provided by State Funds as disaster relief back in the thirties after the old wooden one collapsed in a violent storm. But he was pretty sure the Hook family had lobbied for the bridge.

Serena realised that the County had been all laid out for her, but little about Rick and the Hook family clan themselves not that it particularly worried her, she was with the only one that counted.

'You have a counter plan then?'

He tried to keep it simple. 'I want to transform the County, turn it completely around. This castle would become a casino, hotel and nightclub. Turn the golf course into a professional course, yachting on the lake. Exclusive Nudist beach.' *That was a bit fanciful,* he thought. He spun out the scenario and to Serena's amazement he kept up the flow, interspersed with wine occasionally, for throat lubrication he excused himself. He had Manhandle who was calmly standing in the shadows, get another bottle. And he kept going, in full flight now, pausing only to refill their glasses. 'Do up the shops, have coffee houses, boutiques and stuff, a pleasure come leisure park for families. A nightclub within the casino and four-star suites for the grownups. Put in a pool. Tree planting to disguise the Works from the discerning, the pervading wind blows the smell out to sea thankfully.' By now, the wine was beginning to talk. He hoped he was still making sense and not blathering. He was pleased she liked a drop; it lessened the odds that he would make a fool of himself.

'Good Lord, Rick, you're a visionary. The Peninsular as a gambling, tourist destination and attraction,' cried Serena in admiration as she visualised the scenario.

God damn, he thought, *I am making sense,* he blithered. 'My share, my stake, if you are wondering. Going to sell the Castle, its grounds and most of the peninsular, going to do it real soon. I want to leave this heap of rock.'

Serena thought if this is a heap of rock it was a magnificent heap. 'Rick, you're a genius. Who's the firm arranging the prospectus, brochures, cost analysis and so forth?'

'Well my lawyer, accountant and banker etc.'

'You don't seem at all sure. Look I still have friends who do this type of thing for a living; they could work with your lot.' She thought, *I'm exposing myself back there*, it was a big risk calling in her markers one never knows back in her world whether one is dealing with a Brutus or Brutesses.

Lots of cash would be the key to opening up the resources they would need at such short notice.

'Do you have a computer and stuff?'

Hook replied, 'Got to admit I'm technophobic. All that flashy junk gives me the heebie-jeebies,' and it did, recalling with a shudder his techno hand.

'I want to help truly, leave that type of thing with me, I have contacts,' said Serena with confidence. 'You give me more details and your connections and you and I will knock the socks off the Big Con, what do you say?'

Hook mused, considering her offer. 'Well, you hardly know me, it's a very big ask and it has to happen fast.'

'It will require money, lots of it. Not a problem?' She hoped not, was she gold-digging? Not entirely, she had always liked guys with big ideas and imaginations.

'Hell no honey,' he replied with a laugh. He thought of mentioning the history agenda and its editing right then and there but didn't want to spoil the moment.

'I trust you.' They said simultaneously. They both laughed then having pulled each other's strings and pushed each other's buttons and kissed goodbye.

Serena floated out of the Castle. *Was all this for real? Was she being used?* Of course, she was on reflection, but the payoff could be huge. Her late mother always said, be awake for the main chance and here it was. Her future life beckoned. So what If he was a drinking loony so was she, wasn't she? Was this true love at last?

Chapter 6

Haldenstein still at the pub waited silently as a sentinel. The next move was definitely up to the brothers, he watched as one of them shuffled over to him. 'Hi, me Tic,' it said.

'Haldenstein,' he said putting away his cards and pen and cricking his neck looking up at Tic.

'Hey, come over and join us awhiles, gotta business deal for ya ever.'

Tac made room for Haldenstein at the table. 'Drink?' he asked loudly.

'Gin, large with tonic and ice thank you,' he requested politely but assertively pretending to fiddle with his hearing aid and keeping his eyes on the centre of the messy table. Tic got up and got his order and returned.

'It's like this see, wanta to send out ten or so invites to people we know,' said Tac more softly.

'For a party, you're invited, of course, we would like your fancy writing on them, make them look real nice,' continued Tic.

'Costume party, come as you always wanted to be, free booze, food, music, what have ya ever,' chimed in Tac scratching at his receding chin through his beard.

'Interesting, generous of you both.' said Haldenstein, the smell of them was rank but he had smelt a lot worse. Life for him was gathering pace, first an order from Captain Hook whose father had been subsidising him at the Works. He thought of the Captain and his father; he admired people who could keep a secret at the very least within the family.

'Well, between you and us, it's a farewell party as well, going west directly after.' Tic grinned showing his snaggled orange teeth.

Haldenstein paused, had a drink and slumped back in his seat, massaging his neck as if thinking deeply.

'Take awhile, I take pride in my work, when?' Haldenstein said eventually.

'Soon,' said Tac. 'Got lots to organise first,' he completed, then, 'we are slow movers,' he added.

And thinkers, but devious if not downright cunning as well, thought Haldenstein.

'Payment?'

'We're generous men, what say we give you an advance for cards and stuff? Hey, could you get them delivered as well? $100 cash okay?' asked Tic feeling generous and making a show of reaching into his pocket.

'Deal. Get me the names and address, the balance will be another $50,' said Haldenstein in his terse manner.

'Done,' exclaimed Tic and Tac, both blinking, ticcing and taccing. They sat back and glugged at their drinks in self-congratulation.

'Oh,' said Tic, 'here's a knockout pill for you, if you gotta score to settle, ever haw-haw.'

'Much obliged,' said Haldenstein taking it. *Very useful,* he thought, *just what the doctor ordered.* He smiled to himself, a problem solved.

Chapter 7

Eddie Elwood awoke the next morning, his head ringing and with a deep feeling of dread that made him feel faint and almost rendered him unconscious again. His mobile rang. *Oh Gawd no, here goes,* he thought.

'You're late for work. You get them signs up on the coast, like I ordered,' enquired his work boss, Bedford Wood, nervously.

'Sure did, boss, sorry 'bout being late.'

'Forget it. Signs up, good boy, that covers us ever.' Meaning Bedford himself. 'Some real bad crap going down up there, cops everywhere, evidently. Getting a work gang to fill up that subsidence hole, you can help.'

'Hell, boss, what's going on?' he replied feigning ignorance and listening fearfully. 'Be in soon pronto, boss.' Hoping there weren't any further explanations that involved him.

'Go straight to Charity Point, see you there, alright, right.' The phone rang off, so no further explanations or questions. Elwood stood quivering, shook himself and his mind full of stinking thinking and sweating bullets he made ready to go.

At this point, the weather was clear, fresh from the recent rain with a sharp tang of sea air. Just-about stood apart from the Mayor, the Council Manager and Bedford's work team trying not to call attention to himself, he was acutely aware he may have eaten some important evidence. Crafty Crawford wandered the periphery whistling. He considered putting a road cone on his head as a joke to lighten the general mood but thought better of it and gave it a desultory kick instead. Like a vulture, an ambulance skulked nearby. A big but old wheeled crane commandeered from the Works building site was fishing in the waters off Charity Point for the two cars and their occupants. Jed, the operator of the crane, gave a shout and the steel hawser became taut, slowly what was left of a purple Charger rose to the surface spouting water and seaweed. The crowd grew quiet in anticipation. Skinny Eddie watched with trepidation even though by now he was sure he was in the clear. The purple car was swung around and settled on its chassis with a creak and a groan on the road whereby hundreds of giant crabs fell or leapt out of the car through the smashed windows and scuttled out of the light towards the smell of the sea in front of the horrified crowd who rapidly backed off. The Mainland Sheriff, whose eyes that had seen just about everything moved forward and without ceremony yanked the driver's door open.

The body fell out with the rest of the water. The body was mostly intact, although its eyeless head was virtually skinless, red, green, and its nose and lips missing, long yellow stringy hair was still attached to its scalp. Eyes bulged and watered, stomachs heaved, and the crowd rapidly thinned out.

'Anyone recognises him? It? Yeah, right. The car maybe?' No one spoke up. Most had their eyes cast down or turned away. The Sheriff rolled over what was left of the body with the toe of his boot and carefully pulled out the body's wallet from its back pocket: lots of cash, a Florida driver's licence; Eric Snooks. Not much else was forthcoming.

'Anyone knows an Eric Snooks?' Silence. 'Fetch a blanket,' snarled the Sheriff. The ambulance crew responded and covered up what was left of Leroy. After conferring with the Mayor, the Mainland Sheriff took control; he drew and fired his revolver in the air – there was a stunned silence and the sweet-sour smell of cordite.

'Y'all listen up now. Non-essential personal are ta leave right now,' the Sheriff rasped, 'what ya seen here, stays here, an unfortunate road accident in the line of duty.' He looked hard at a freaked-out white-faced Serena with her reporter credentials pinned to her chest.

'This aint no light joke, remember the crabs and the trouble last time,' loudly proclaimed the Mayor and gave Serena an equally hard look. Jed continued fishing for the other car. Sheriff Guber's patrol car came up and was swung around, a water-inflated Stars and Stripe condom swung from its radio antennae to the mystification of the onlookers' and then water and crabs streamed burst out the doors as it landed near the Charger. The smaller apprehensive crowd waited expectantly. Some of the less hardy stepped well away.

'No one in here,' announced the ambulance crew with relief. The condom burst into the crowd's stymied disbelief; was this some sort of denigration of the Flag? The crane gave a sudden shudder and a loud thud as both its hand and air brakes failed and it sailed majestically backwards over the cliff, the attached Sheriff's car a wingless sailplane flying out behind it. Jed jumped clear with a terrified shriek.

The crowd stood milling around in an uncomprehending mob then heeding the Sheriff's warning, dispersed to their cars; most left muttering dire predictions for the future.

'Well, so long Galoot, it's been no good to know you,' muttered Deputy Early, which was the closest Sheriff Guber ever got to having a eulogy.

'Deputy Early over here,' ordered Mayor Botox Clone standing by the large shadow of the Mainland Sheriff. 'This here is Sheriff Sawyer, he will be our acting County Sheriff till you and we get our act together or ever.' Mayor whispered in his ear, 'over there they call him the Sweeper.' For a second, Just-about thought he said reaper, but he cringed anyway. Sheriff Sawyer came up real close. He wore a black Stetson uniform that matched his narrow eyes. In one of his massive scarred hands, he lightly carried his mirror shades; a smouldering cigar hung from the corner of his slit of a mouth. His gun looked like it had seen plenty of action like the face of the owner. He was far bigger, meaner and harder looking than even the late unlamented Guber. He exuded menace and business; he was a dark storm of a man who looked like he could spit lightning. Just-about almost lost his gun belt again.

Chapter 8

'Well, I'll be, would ya believe it!' hollered Tic to Tac who was in the other room. 'The Sheriffs bought the farm and probably cus Leroy by the description of one of the cars. No loss there. Probably not a real cousin anyway.' Tic held up the Peninsular Advocate he only read for the funnies and its headline: *TRAGEDY AT CHARITY POINT*, and pointing.

Tac squinted and reading the front page of the paper slowly; grunted, 'Well, one less on our list, pity. No connection to us and our plans at all. Let's lay low till this cloud of crap passes over awhiles anyway, use the old Chevy in town for now.' Tic nodded in agreement.

'Gruder thought he was so smart he could pogo stick across quicksand.' Laughed Tic with Tac joining in.

But then disappointment etched both their ugly faces, they had wanted Guber for themselves. They thought of compensation.

'There is only one thing for it.' They donned their slaughter gear. 'The brown spotted pig, I think, barbecued pork chops tonight, yum-yum.' They both smacked their lips. 'Keep the blood and guts etc. in the new fridge for blood pudding and ever.' They laughed, winking, ticking and tacking at each other both Leroy and the Sheriff forgotten.

Chapter 9

Captain Hook was being unusually decisive. With help from Serena, he had assembled perspective, hard-on facts for the money changers and lenders, and lots of gloss and glamour for the less discerning. The Castle Casino, Night Club and Hotel were the major thrust of the document. Embedded in the documents were the sale of the castle and its eighty acres of cultivated parks and gardens. To protect Hook's staff, the gatehouse with its own small bit of land was not for sale. The Conglomerate was being given an opportunity to make gold – it was almost too good to be true. The beef market faded in significance against the land value. With help from Serena's friends, the Scheme was a remarkable arm-twisting masterpiece. Unusual in that it was totally candid with no fish hooks even a hard-ass banker, accountant or lawyer would ever find because there was none. The financial spreadsheet was a marvel of precision, showing beautiful beautiful profits, it was an investor's wet dream. All that was needed was a date for an acceptance meeting with Castle as the obvious venue.

On the debit side, the Captain was still to have Serena help him with editing his family and the Peninsula's peculiar history, perhaps a little subterfuge was required. This particular mission was an obsession for sure, but a man's got to have some point to his life, right? And as of late, he had been having disturbing dreams, in them, he saw himself dressed as a surgeon lancing a large boil that was the Castle. Perhaps it was post-traumatic stress disorder manifesting itself, perhaps it was because it was the first time in an age he had given his brain a workout?

Chapter 10

Tic and Tac had not been idle either, from their letterbox an old beer cask on its side out at the dead gate, they retrieved a heavy cardboard box that jangled and a large rectangular envelope. Back in their lair, they opened the box. Out fell ten large handcuffs and keys. From Hold-Tite Delite Co Ltd, Charleston read an enclosed card.

'Well done, mail order, ya could order the whole of America from it,' said Tic. Tac grinned. They opened the envelope and there in almost new condition were two Alabama car number plates.

'It pays to have friends like Ugly Auntie,' they said. They moved through to the slaughter room, pulling the heavy tarp apart at the centre with a chain. Along the side wall was a stainless steel bench with troughs and sinks at one end with drains leading outside to the offal pit in the paddock and through the creek to the general bog. Arranged on the bench were cleavers, boning knives and other butchering gear and a large unusual electric chainsaw. They splattered red paint over the lot and the walls to enhance the overall effect. It looked hellish as they intended. The remainder of the paint they used on their 4x4, painting bonnet and tailgate red. They removed the gun racks, bull bars and extra lights and fixed the new old number plates in place.

Back inside, an overhead steel beam ran across the room. From it hung at regular intervals were the steel hooks recently purloined from the Meat Works. 'Great isn't it, near the end of the party we pull the tarp apart and there for all them to see will be all the body meat hung upside down on the hooks,' said Tac. 'All blood and guts, teach those sons of bitches to fic with us, what a hoot, then we lic outta here, sweet home Alabama, Ugly Auntie here we come.'

They looked out the window; a happy suckling piglet was scrambling around doing figures of eight. 'Cute and tasty too I bet. How many gobblers and pigs including all those little piggies we got?' Both thinking of Thanksgiving Day and their stomachs. They counted, then again. Twenty-six all up they agreed.

'On the 26th,' they said in unison. The twenty-sixth was unique, it was Celebration Day, it should have been an anniversary but no one could agree on or remember the particulars so it was declared an official Public Holiday on 25th on the Peninsular anyway. It at least dated back to when Thanksgiving Day the 22nd continued onwards as a five-day event and this year would be no different and it was coming up fast.

'Seriously tho.' After they returned to the main room. 'This new Sheriff may be the real thing. From now on we get our booze and stuff from the Mainland and drink here,' said Tic.

'Sure, besides that crap TV at the back bar is so small I don't know whether I'm watching pro wrestling or a porno

112

movie,' replied Tac, 'one more trip to see Haldenstein and that's that, right?'

'Right.'

They met Haldenstein at the pub as arranged. The invites were ready. 'Okay, it starts four-thirty, Monday the 26th of November, the Public Holiday. You still want me to deliver them?' asked Haldenstein taking the list and addresses.

'Yeah on both counts.'

Haldenstein got to work while the brothers guzzled and gurgled. He paid particular attention to the one to Dr Mengele. It was both flattering and cajoling. 'Great, invite yaself,' said the brothers admiringly.

Haldenstein said, 'You already have. I've taken the liberty to make you a sign to put on the bar as well, more the merrier right?'

The brothers read it, thought for a moment, 'What the hell, it's as ya say, the more the merrier.' Unintentionally, the sign made their hit list nearly redundant and once the news was out, they could expect a greedy crowd anyway, lovely.

Haldenstein gathered up the invites collected the balance of his money and headed out to his other appointment. He met Captain Hook in his limo as arranged. 'Two Canadian Passports and visas as requested, Captain, made out to Mr and Mrs Hyde. Here, you keep your old passport,' he said as he handed it over. 'I have taken the liberty to have Switz visas, other requirements, your entry date etc. into Switzerland stamped in it. You will need it to offer it for identification at your bank when you get there.'

'Good heavens, you've thought of everything. Thank you, unbelievable, how much do I owe, do you need anything?'

'Nix, I'm very well set.' Smiled Haldenstein. 'As you probably know, your father helped me in Germany forty-five when things were very dire and later here, good luck in your endeavours, Captain, goodbye.' The Captain's eyes were strangely moist on Haldenstein's departure; this connection with his late father was broken.

Previously, the Captain had sent off a trunk of the Peninsula's history and the family stuff to the Baur au Lac Hotel in Zurich pending the arrival of a Mr and Mrs Hyde. What if she said no to the history editing? There was no backup plan. It was all or nothing. He was backing his instincts and hoping providence was on his side.

Haldenstein returned to his cottage and wound up his hidden wireless aerial. He retrieved his cypher book from its hiding place, took up the Writings and flicked to the words on Job. Then set up his secret wireless with its pre-tuned frequency; when it was well warmed up, he radioed his concentration camp number. There was a brief pause; he could almost hear the powerful high-speed computers whirling. 'Shalom,' a distant voice said.

'Shalom,' replied Haldenstein. He continued in code, 'Come most urgently to view and verify body of…' he spoke the code name of the SS Doktor and gave them were and the 27th as the date. 'I repeat…'

'The Unspoken and we bless you out,' was the swift reply.

He turned off then smashed the radio and aerial to smithereens with a hatchet, burnt the cypher book and the

Writings then buried the lot very deep within his vacationing neighbour's overgrown vegetable patch.

Part 3

Chapter 1

Sheriff Sawyer was determined to make his mark in Monsterville USA before he returned to the real world of the Mainland. First, he had a sign made up. With it he marched into the Thistle Inn, sat down in a booth with the sign displayed at the end of the table, it read: *TEMPORARY SHERIFF'S OFFICE – Open 12 to half past: Saturdays only.*

He ordered a large whisky straight and drank it down in one gulp. 'Another, much larger,' he rasped. The bar fell into a stunned silence. 'Music, country and western, softly,' he ordered. 'And turn off that cursed TV.' Harvard Huckleberry rushed to comply. Slowly, conversation returned to the bar. A genuine hard bastard was Gloria's summation. She sidled over to the Sheriff's booth and slid into the opposite bench seat.

'Ya,' said the Sherriff barely looking up from his drink.

'See that bald skinny guy over there in the Council overalls?' sneered Gloria with malice short-circuiting her brain and her heart at half-mast.

'Yeah.'

'Him's names Eddie and he's bin peeping tomming in ma windows at night.'

'Positive?'

'Ya.'

The sheriff carefully drew on his black leather gloves. 'Wait here,' he ordered. He strode over to the hapless Eddie and pulled him up out of his seat by the scruff of his neck and poking him in both eyes viciously with his spread fingers whispered into Eddie Elwood's ear. 'No more peeking at night, leave her alone, got it?' He pushed Skinny Eddie back in his seat.

With his hands over his eyes blubbing Eddie sobbed, 'Never have, never did, wouldn't did.' All of this happened to be true, Elwood had enough; in despair, he went home to his workshop and took down from the wall his late father's large Bowie knife and started his metal grinder, with goggles and gloves on he started grinding away; sparks and steel flew... Time passed, he stopped; he looked down in consternation and amazement, he had whittled away the blade till nothing was left except a very long misshapen stiletto.

At the pub, the Law eyes had followed Skinny Eddie out the door; he grimaced and then returned to his seat. Sawyer stared hard at Gloria and scowled darkly. 'That's *your* last complaint, move your ugly ass,' he grunted returning to his drink. Chastised for probably the first time ever, Gloria abashed, returned to her stool. Sawyer's next customer was Scmelling.

'It's me neighbour,' and he poured out the same story he had relayed to Captain Hook. Scmelling had suffered a serious blackout and a horrendous hangover from all the Scotch and consequently his mind had boggled and he had completely forgotten he had been to the Castle let alone seen Hook.

'I see,' said Sherriff Sawyer, he turned his sign over on the table. 'Come with me,' he said and marched Scmelling to his squad car. 'Sit in the back,' he commanded.

'Am I arrested?' Gulped Scmelling, wishing he hadn't approached the Sheriff in the first place, he suddenly felt like he was about to shat a fat chicken he regaled some good old boys later.

'Not this time, what's the name of this peace disrupter and his address?'

Scmelling gave him the information, so on this soft aired Saturday, in no time they pulled up the drive of Schelling's neighbour. Sheriff Sawyer delved into his car's glove box and finally found an old pad, wrote on a form and signed it, then tore it off.

'Keep out of sight,' he ordered Schelling. He then marched up to the front door and knocked loudly three times. A fit-looking guy, a foot shorter than Sawyer wearing jeans and a white tee shirt opened the door. 'Noise Abatement Notice served,' said Sawyer shoving the form into the man's hand, 'let's see the offending noise makers on the front lawn right now, please.'

The flabbergasted owner, still reading the complicated form and its fine print, complied, not really knowing what was going on but Sawyer's hand on his gun convinced him to get on with it. In a neat row, he laid out a lawnmower, hedge clippers, weed eater, chainsaw and lastly the water-blaster. Sawyer went to the back of the squad car and out of the trunk produced a heavy sledge hammer he normally used to smash open front doors, marched over to the machines and began pounding them to pieces watched by the incredulous owner and Scmelling who was peeping over the car's window watching with unbelieving eyes. Sheriff Sawyer stopped. 'Thank you for your co-operation, sir.' Turned about with one hand on his gun and got back in the car and drove to the Thistle Inn and dropped off the pop-eyed Smelling who couldn't wait to tell all and sundry at the bar what he had witnessed, just as the sheriff intended but first he hurried to the toilets.

Next, Sheriff Sawyer drove to the opposite side of the peninsular and the Meat Works where he encountered a van leaving the works; he pulled it over. The plump, dough-faced driver with a pug nose was understandably nervous looking at the approaching figure with its silver star on its massive chest and black mirror sunglasses down over its eyes.

'Loading docket please,' ordered Sawyer leaning on the van's window sill.

'Sorry, Sheriff, must have misplaced it,' said the driver hastily pretending to look for it his jowls quivering.

'Bullshit out,' ordered Sawyer. 'Van door, open,' he continued. The driver hurried to comply by sliding back the side door. 'Well, well, what is all this then and no loading docket, tut-tut?' Revealed were a heap of large faucets, lead waste pipes and miscellaneous taps and stainless steel pipes.

'Naughty, very naughty, now a *kind* man would call this pilfering another looting.' He turned to the now red-faced craven driver. 'Looting carries a much heavier sentence.'

The driver still had his hand on the open side of the van door. Sawyer slammed the door back on the driver's six-fingered hand. His scream of pain could have been heard on the opposite side of the Peninsular.

'Now whatever your name is, spread the word, pilfering from the works I call looting, take this load of stuff back before I consider charging you with the same, got it?'

'Yes sir,' whimpered the driver through tears of cringing pain.

'Here have this,' said the Sheriff thrusting out a flat object.

The driver automatically held out his uninjured hand and the powerful rat trap slammed shut on it. 'Goodbye present, bye now,' said the Sheriff as he stalked to his car leaving the driver bent over wringing his hands and stamping round in circles cursing. *Such a big vocabulary for such a little man*, thought Sawyer. He returned to his office and made some phone calls, worked on the computer, received faxes and gathered further information, then went out and bought a pair of heavy men's work braces and a plastic pink raincoat. Back in the office, he rang the Works Manager C J and told to him to get extra security guards to man the gates checking outward goods and vehicles or he would be arrested for Aiding and Abetting as well as being an Accessory after the fact and anything else he was sure to think of. He heard a bout of nervous coughing as he put down the phone not bothering to wait for a reply.

The sheriff leaned back in his chair and lit up his cigar, plonked his black crocodile cowboy boots cross-ankled up on the desk and called in Early.

'Stand easy, Early.' Early had his gun belt cinched so tight he looked like an hourglass. 'These strong braces are yours, what you do is wear them high and tight. On your gun

123

belt, you fasten fish hooks and you hang your gun belt on your trousers, then you put on your jacket git it.'

Early smiled for the first time in days. 'Yes sir, Sheriff sir.'

'Don't call me sir, I work for a living. What do you know about those big, ugly brothers?'

'Well, their ancestors ate flies and in the Civil—'

'Heard it,' interrupted the Sheriff.

'Geronimo?'

'Hogwash,' barked the Sheriff.

'When Paul Revere road forward warning the British were comin a gullible retard from the town with English coins in his pocket rode around bellowing, "The British aint coming!"'

'Dang dog dirt and drivel,' snarled the exasperated Sheriff. 'Forget it, snap out of it, Deputy. Listen up, it's time to make your mark around this shite hole I won't be here forever, thank Gawd.'

He handed over the pink plastic raincoat. 'You give this to Bald Maud to wear in the mornings, say it's from a secret admirer who doesn't want her to catch a cold, be very persuasive and insistent, also tell her to get a blue wig her secret *rich admirer really likes* blue ones.' A corner of his mouth turned up slightly and was swiftly gone. 'Now that giant in behind her in the Lotto come Video store is an Illegal alien. He's a wanted man, a Mexican wrestler called Oscar Gonzales, done more assault, battering and bloody mayhem outside the ring than in it. You're to notify the Immigration Authorities quickly before he does another runner and have them arrest him. Let them deal with it. Also,' the Sweeper continued, 'the Lotto owner is technoscamming the Lotto Grid. Call the Gaming Commission and tell them right away. On arrival of the Gaming Inspectors, arrest the cross-eyed son of a bitch Lotto prick and throw the book at him. Get this right you may make sheriff yet.' Though he thought Early had fat farts to hope in hell of that. 'Walk tall, Deputy,' encouraged the Sheriff. 'Get the belt fixed first, though. Dismiss.'

Deputy Early wafted out the door with a grin as wide as his waist. Behind him, Sawyer wondered why those two slaughtermen had gone to the ground. The Mayor was a mine of information and the grapevine in the town well watered except on this point and Early had been no help. He relit his cigar; they didn't call him the Sweeper for nothing, now to wait for the next wheelbarrow full of crap coming over the pike, if the uglies were pushing it or anyone else they were in for a big surprise. If he only knew what was coming, the Sweeper would have gone out and bought a very big broom indeed.

Chapter 2

Manhandle brought Hook his mail, the contents made the Captain smile in satisfaction. There were two certificates stating the holders were signed up for Marriage Celebrants and two Marriage Certificates. One for Richard Hook, the other made out to Michael Manhandle. All signed and correct. There were some instructions on their use. Money has its uses. He put them aside for the time being, all he had to do was sign one and Michael Manhandle the other to make them both legitimate.

Captain Hook had called a staff meeting out in the portico. For him, it was going to be something of an ordeal; he decided to keep the news short and to the point. When Manhandle, Marie and Millie had seated themselves he started, 'Not everything lasts forever,' he began lamely. Marie and Millie looked at the ground in alarm, Manhandle tried to catch the Captain's elusive eyes. 'I'm leaving here for good on Monday the 26th November the Peninsula's Public Holiday, next week in fact, after Thanksgiving Day. Never coming back, ever. My destination is unknown at this stage.' Millie started crying.

He put his hand on her shoulder. 'I'm sorry everyone for the short notice, but everything changes nothings perfect.'

AIN'T NOBODY PERFECT either, he thought. Manhandle held Marie's hand and squeezed softly.

God, this is more difficult than he envisaged. 'Events beyond my control have determined our future,' he said trying to keep it inclusive, which was harder than he thought. *Be more positive man, loosen up,* he castigated himself.

He spoke more positively, 'Millie, you can return to Samoa a rich woman to do whatever you desire. I know you have a large extended family; you can give them all a better future. Is that what you want?'

Millie looked up at him with tears in her eyes. 'Yes, but I will miss being here. I've been very happy here.'

'And I'll miss you too,' said the Captain sincerely. 'We'll talk about details later.'

'Michael, my dear friend, when are going to make an honest woman out of Marie?'

Manhandle put an arm around Marie. They smiled at each other, then at the Captain.

'Before you leave, Captain,' promised Manhandle speaking for both the lovers.

'The Gatehouse keep and its immediate grounds I have bequeathed to you both if you want to stay, but if not, you can sell it off. You will both receive a generous gratuity. Details again later, okay? Hey, cheer up you three, you won't have to wait on this silly odd fart anymore.' He continued, 'Please keep this conversation secret won't you?' He poured four glasses of champagne.

'A toast to us,' he said standing up. The threesome followed.

'To us and a new happy and prosperous future.' They clinked glasses.

'It's not the end of the world,' he said cheerfully as he could as he completed the little ceremony and went inside with his glass leaving the bottle and another for the staff and a chance to ponder and talk to each other in private.

Before Manhandle left, the Captain called him aside. 'Michael, do you still have contact with your old comrades in the Army Engineers? That lifer up in the Blue Ridge Mountains, for instance, what's he up to?'

'On Bear Bluff, called O'Hagan, he still looks after that old Army munitions dump, makes moonshine he trades with any hillbilly who crosses his path, drinks most of it himself. Raises a few goats and sheep.' He paused then, 'A forgotten man. Still receives his pay checks into his bank so he doesn't mind much.'

'Just checking he's still around. Quite a character, as you say, stocks Army Engineer explosives, blasts the river occasionally for fish, right?'

'Sure, Rick, what's up?'

Rick told him the score, it took him a while. Manhandle listened intently with disbelief; had his friend finally gone completely loopy? The Captain passed over Manhandle's Wedding Celebrant Certificate. 'I've got one too, you marry me and Serena, and I marry you and Marie Monday morning the 26th, what you say?'

Manhandle digested this information carefully, then. 'That's on the Peninsula's Public Holiday. A bit of a rush Richard but okay.' He signed the proffered document. 'What makes you think Serena will marry you? You've just met.'

Rick laughed. 'A diamond ring as big as a lump of coal.'

***

Hook got on the phone with Serena. 'Hi there, busy tonight?'

'In this place! What have you got in mind? Oh, dinner at your place? Formal, well okay.'

'Best Peninsular steak as a main.'

'Super, about what time?'

'Manhandle will pick you up about seven thirty, is that alright?'

'Great.'

'Okay, then looking forward to seeing you.'

'Me too.'

Chapter 3

The Sheriff read the sign on the bar of the Thistle Inn, it had the makings of big trouble. He asked Sweet Sylvester about it. 'The brothers Grimm, Tic and Tac are throwing a bash out at Lone Oak. They won biggish at Lotto. Should be fun but probably damn weird as well, I got a fancy invite.' Looking happy but a bit puzzled. He hoped the brothers were dressed up with their faces covered if not he would pretend they were dressed as large werewolves. In the town and the Works, very similar thoughts had crossed many minds but the allure of free booze and food overcame their misgivings – and it was a *farewell* party thank the Lord, no more being scared shitless at the sight of them.

'Where is Lone Oak?'

'Their place, bit of a barn out in the boondoggle.'

The Sheriff thought translating, out in the countryside. Except for an urgent call, he would stay well away. His presence would only fuel any possible fire. From bitter experience, he knew it was better to let a wildfire burn out and sift through the dead embers for any evidence of wrongdoing the next day.

Chapter 4

Serena arrived at the castle in due time in a splendid emerald full-length evening gown, the colour matching her eyes, all of which took Hook's breath away, her red hair was let down and she wore red pumps to match. Minimal jewellery, minimal make-up, she had small freckles across her petit nose he hadn't noticed before. He bowed. He was dressed in his full formal Highland regalia. 'Well,' said Serena, 'aren't we both dandies.'

Captain Hook beamed brightly. 'All very fitting for the occasion, Serena,' he said.

Michael Manhandle was dressed as a maitre de in a black tuxedo with a tartan sash around his waist, Marie was their waitress in black with white lace trim befitting a manor house hovered differently behind Manhandle. 'This way my lady,' flourished Manhandle.

He led the couple to a banquet room off to one the side of the main hall. The room was fitted with a plush burgundy coloured carpet, tapestries hung on the walls and a chandelier was lit low in deference to a silver candelabrum aglow with candles. A subtle Bach variation played in the background. White Rocco-inspired menus sat erect at each end of the polished maple table dressed in the centre by red roses in a Ming vase. Manhandle pulled out a chair for the dazed Serena. Captain Hook helped himself to the other. Manhandle withdrew a Dom Perignon from the crested ice bucket and from a nod by the Captain, opened it with professional sharp but careful pop and frothed two glasses.

'A toast,' declared the Captain after the froth had settled raising his crystal flute. They were the first words spoken since they entered the room.

'This is too much.' Smiled Serena. 'What are we toasting?'

'Us, and a match made in heaven,' replied the Captain hopefully, his medals sparkling. They ordered. There was little talk. For the first time in her life, Serena was tongue-tied. She allowed herself with mounting pleasure to be seduced. After the four-course meal, the Captain rose and gently led her to an adjacent bedroom with its vast four-poster bed. Both of them were fully aware the minute they walked into the banquet room that this was to be the culmination of the evening. Sometime during the night, the music changed from Bach to Wagner, and the Valerie's came and bore her away. That hook was a magic wand. They were compatible with a capital 'C'.

The next morning, Serena awoke to songbirds. Kneeling at her bedside was the Captain wearing a silk dressing gown. In his hand, he proffered her a gold box. She in amazement, opened it. Inside, nestling in velvet, was a diamond ring; its proportions magnificent. She felt tears of joy spring to her eyes. 'Please,' he said with an anxious smile.

'Yes,' she said and opened the silk bed linen to let him back in. So bliss was still available in this stuffed-up world, after all, they both thought as one. Theirs was indeed a match made in heaven.

Chapter 5

If Serena and Rick's match was made in heaven, Tic and Tac's was made in Dante's inferno. They had made numerous trips to the Mainland and had deliveries made. They had cleaned up the barn and the slaughter room was made ready for the big night. They set up the hi-fi system and the copious amounts of food and bags of ice were ready in the large fridge. They tried on their surgical outfits and masks and had a good laugh. Haw-haw, hee-hee, they went.

The Costume Hire outfit at Travis City did a roaring trade around morning and lunchtime and early in the afternoon of the 26th. Clowns, cops, nurses, pirates, devils and animal outfits were popular. A couple hired biker gear, black, complete with silver chains and what have you for he and she. An elderly man with obviously dyed blonde hair came in for a Nazi uniform and was put out with the only officer's uniform available. 'The ranks too low,' he muttered but took it all the same. A small skinny guy hired a Superman outfit.

'Good luck to you on that one.' The counter staff laughed. And so it went. *Mind you, it was a public holiday over on the Peninsular,* they thought enviously, *must be some big costume party,* they reasoned correctly.

Chapter 6

The Castle household had been busy as well, a large truck arrived with poker machines, blackjack tables, roulette wheels and other gambling paraphernalia which were uncommissioned as of yet and were mostly for show. The colourful wares were skilfully arranged around the reception room by a high-flying consultant as if all were ready to spring into action at a moment's notice. A temporary bar was set up and a long banquet table was set in the middle and a large business table was placed handily nearby against a wall complete with the relevant contract documents and a couple of expensive Mont Blanc pens were left casually lying around. The business plan, and a coloured brochure with before and after pictures, a map of the Peninsular, plans of the castle, figures etc., having been sent out previously to the Big Con and other interested parties and officials who had approved the plans in principle. Large coloured reproductions of the plans by reputable interior designers and architects were mounted on the wall above the business table.

An Insurance firm had rung Hook. Yes, the Castle was insured, he had cancelled the policy that morning and yes it had water sprinklers and smoke alarms. Rick did not mention the ones upstairs had been turned off. Yes, he would follow that up in writing from his Insurers, yes, they could trust him to do so. He had no intention of doing any of it. It was all on then. Only the signing remained. On the big day was set to start at six o'clock, there would be a serious smorgasbord manned by hired staff as would be the bar. They were set for a big night. Interesting, the stairs to the top floor and battlements were roped off with signs politely saying, *Upgrading work underway please do not venture further.*

Chapter 7

The Peninsular Public Holiday arrived on a still day with little fanfare, flags, banners and bunting still hung limply down the length of Main Street. Most of the town was satiated from Thanksgiving Day and the already long weekend. The majority of the population were sleeping in conserving their energy for the later in the day traditional flare up and this year, the Costume Party was an added distraction from the pending Works closure before some sort of normality resumed. The Sheriff was called out to a domestic around lunchtime. An unhappy drunk decided he rather carve up his wife than a leftover turkey. The wife was unhurt and the culprit of the mini-mayhem now paced a cell moaning in remorse; otherwise, the day and town were mostly quiet as if it was gearing up for something big.

Sheriff Sawyer stared banefully out his window facing onto Main Street. Except for the party out at Lone Oak, there seemed no cause for alarm. There was some do up at the Castle but he presumed it would be a genteel affair, nevertheless, his gut instincts told him differently. All he could do was wait but he put his deputy on alert without explanation. Deputy Early was disappointed; he was hoping to go to the party as Marshal Wyatt Earp with his newfound confidence in wearing a gun.

***

Earlier that day, a small happy affair took place at the Gatehouse of the Castle, Michael Manhandle married Marie Gonzales, Captain Hook officiating and Richard Hook married Sarah Parsons with Michael officiating. Sarah nee Serena had come clean with Rick on her name. Rick said Sarah suited her better giving her a tender hug. The others were surprised and somewhat baffled but did not let it spoil the occasion after Rick gave them a brief but very plausible explanation. Sarah suspected that Rick knew anyway which he did. Millie Brown and Randy the Ranch Manager were the witnesses on both occasions.

After the ceremony, the signing and Randy's departure, Rick took Sarah aside.

'How do feel about a honeymoon in Switzerland, we are all booked, I know it's a precipitant, I hope you will forgive me.'

'Gee,' said Sarah as she was now known, 'you *are* a fast worker, I can't tell you not to do it again because you probably would, besides I like big surprises.'

'Yes, but sorry anyway for not giving you a choice, but I have urgent business in Zurich. Two birds with one stone kind of thing. We fly by my private Jet from here, off the golf course as matter of fact.'

Sarah looked at Rick in consternation. 'What's up, Rick, come clean with your wife,' she demanded. So he did. She took it all with surprisingly good grace considering the work she had put into his Conglomerate plan. 'And you want me to help with the editing of your families and the Peninsular history and so forth?'

'Well, yes, but you see there's no time limit, more of a hobby, we can't spend the rest of our lives in bed and at play,' he said smoothly.

'I'm okay with the editing, enjoy it even. When do we leave?'

Rick gave a deep sigh of relief. 'Late this afternoon, after the Casino negotiations etc., not that there is much to negotiate, mostly signings.'

'This is getting more like a strange alternative script to "Casablanca", Rick. But I have no ties here. The adventure of a lifetime. Must hurry and pack.' *Half a sqillion dollars if things turned to custard,* she thought. There had been no prenuptial rubbish; so she trusted him and anyway she really did love the guy – well maybe. She had nothing to lose and everything to gain. A new start, she was now a wanted woman in the States so she had heard recently from friends. *With that touch of larceny in her,* she thought, *game on my dear Rick.*

'Don't pack much, the shopping in Zurich is splendid. Oh, by the way, we will be Mr and Mrs Hyde, hide with a "y" en route, over there and beyond.'

'Holy shit, Rick,' was the only thing she could think of to say.

Chapter 8

Tic and Tac were excited and dressed as surgeons were booze cruising and going bananas over the turnout. The locusts had descended, and the barn was full. It was just a matter of choosing and Tic and Tac were spoilt for choice. It was going on six, early, yet the party was well and truly alight, if not ablaze. The music was raucously loud, they had none to gently persuade a Leroy look alike from the Works to man the gram and who was now staring agog at the weird wonders around him. People were going haywire on the lethal punch, literately climbing the walls, dancing frenetically, rock and rolling to Elvis and Little Richards or jiving and generally twisting themselves out of shape or zonging and were generally out of control on the lethal alcohol and drug mixture.

Scmelling, his face blackened as the twenties or something shoeshine boy was making a nuisance of himself going around on all fours trying to polish people's shoes. Hedy as Dolly Parton was standing on a hay bale making plaintive whinin', cryin' and squealing noises singing country songs into a chicken leg thinking it was mike. Chief Bluebluff his face smeared in full war paint on High Kick was whooping it up. C J the Works Manager, the large wart on his forehead glowing like a Christmas light came dressed as a cowboy. Astride a hay bale, he kept hollering, 'get along little doggy,' and was given a beady look from Tic and Tac as was Sweet Sylvester who came dressed as Cinderella. Gloria was all dressed up in her most revealing and sensual work clothes; black and red suspender belt, net stockings, the works, was cracking a whip while trying to make eye contact with any female who came near, they in turn avoided her like the plague. Skinny Eddie as Superman was giving her looks of pure hateful lust.

Bald Maude wearing a blue wig and her pink raincoat was twirling an umbrella aloft as Mary Poppins and flashing her old-fashioned undies while skipping girlishly around looking for her secret rich admirer. Editor Larryoe Lowell as a diminutive Abe Lincoln in a fierce political debate with himself was angrily jumping up and down on his stovepipe hat. Two locals dressed up as a biker couple were having a fight with two real Mainland gate crashing bikers who much to their surprise were coming off second best. Chaos reigned.

Dozens of dancing dervishes danced out of rhythm to Jerry Lee Lewis. Scores of singers sang out of tune with Fats Domino. Many were prone on hay bales and out of it early on, one a devil, lay prostrate on one with an evil grin on his face zonging and thinking he was either in Sodom or Gomorrah was twitching from time to time to the music which he saw as leaping yellow-red flames, glowing coals and smouldering embers.

Boo Coley dressed as a priest imploringly raised his hands up to heaven and bellowed a sermon to save these here wicked folk for they do not know what they do which was true for ninety percent of them. Tac wacked Fiery Fred the Works Foreman supine with a baseball bat when Fred dressed as a fireman turned nasty as usual. The Works Paymaster as Santa Clause sat giggly his ass stuck in the trough much to the annoyance of Tic. 'Fic off, Santa, go play with your elves and gnomes ever,' Tic said ominously into his ear. Santa moved off with Tic following in slow measured pursuit. A clown with a huge red grin on his face vomited into his friend's pirate hat. A brief food fight broke out, wild laughter everywhere.

Dr Mengele arrived thinking he was splendid in his black Nazi uniform and swastika armband. Ironic Seig Heil's broke out, Mengele by now not knowing what was real and what was not, with pleasure gave the straight-armed Nazi salute to the motley crowd. *So, it was worth the risk,* he thought helping himself to a drink from a half-empty bottle of vodka. Haldenstein crept in, in his original concentration camp clothes and striped cap. Back in those most terrible of days, he was grateful to even have a cap.

Tic and Tac administered a knockout pill to Cinderella and dragged him through the tarp along with Santa Clause and the Cowboy who had also been given the treatment. They were stripped and hung upside down with handcuffs by their ankles, legs spread apart to the hooks hanging from the steel beam. The music played on. Haldenstein approached Dr Mengele head-on.

'Mein Gott,' spluttered the Doctor, 'the Cockroach is surely a Jude as always I thought so!'

'Prost, Herr Doktor Mengele, torturer and mass murderer. I see you have been demoted,' said Haldenstein condenscendly. He held up his glass. Mengele was deeply insulted and his overwhelming pride hurt. He almost lost it right there and then but at the last moment stiffened himself. He had a quick look around; some semi-sober people close by were watching them. His gun in its black leather holster was a block of wood, *a pity*, he cursed to himself, his eyes blazing red below the brim of his cap with its Deaths Head insignia.

'To reconciliation,' snarled the wounded Mengele insincerely, trying to smile without much success for the small audience nearby. He clicked his jackboots together. They touched glasses. Haldenstein unseen, with his quick and nimble fingers, dropped his knock-out pill into the doctor's glass.

Back behind the tarp curtain, Tic and Tac went to the new fridge and came back with the recently slaughtered pig's blood and guts in buckets. They hung intestines over the crutches of their first three victims and generously ladled pig's blood over everything so it was covering their bodies and dripping down from their heads, they looked guttered. Very realistic, they both thought in admiration of their work.

Haldenstein who had been carefully watching Tic and Tac dragged a comatose Mengele through the tarp. 'My contribution,' he said on entering. Tic and Tac winked at Haldenstein and undressed Mengele and strung him upside down with the rest. While Tic and Tac were engaged, Haldenstein picked up the large electric chainsaw and plugged it in and turned on the switch. The brothers bent down for the pig stuff. Haldenstein in one unbelievably strong and revengeful stroke cut Mengele in two; groin to head.

'Whats youse done!' screamed Tac in genuine horror and tearing off his surgical mask ran to the long drop and bending over, started vomiting down its reeking hole.

Back at the party, Skinny Eddie with his hand behind his back moved towards Gloria near the rear straw bales and then faced her. One kind word even then may have saved her, but no.

'Well, if it's not super-dickhead,' she scoffed with a sneer. Skinny Eddie through a descending red mist saw her for what she really was – a succubus, a demon. He drove the long Bowie stiletto, now a glowing red hot poker sizzling into her solar plexus and up into her heart. She suddenly smiled at him; a sad dying smile, it was as if he had freed her from bondage. Abruptly the mist cleared and she fell forwards into him and then slid down onto the floor. He wrestled out the knife and threw it under the tarp then cradled her tenderly and kissed her.

'Just one kind word, just one small gesture would have done.' He started to weep. The music played on.

Tic stood glaring at Haldenstein and in outrage cried, 'The Family aint done that sorta thing since 1962! It's meant ta be a huge farewell bloody joke, a ficcing scary laugh!' He grabbed the chainsaw off Haldenstein, and the iffy cord slid along the wet floor. The resulting electric shock staggered him around the room and the chainsaw still roaring disappeared up Tac's perfectly positioned rectum. The grotesque tableau shook, smoked and sparked blue and white so ending Tic and Tac's lineage. Haldenstein grabbed the chain and parted the tarpaulin, and then the man in the striped pyjamas slipped out the rear door into the slowly gathering dusk. Someone summoning up their last iota of sense called the Sheriff. The music stopped.

Chapter 9

Earlier the Sheriff from his office window watched with suspicion as a small fleet of flash cars with a limousine leading made their way past him and snaked up the hill to the castle. Another limo from the opposite direction pulled up across the street. A car passed by with a grinning clown at the wheel and a leering pirate beside him with Cinderella in the back. Then another with a variety of animals with a gorilla driving. *Just when you thought you had seen it all,* thought the Sheriff but recalling the sign in the pub and its heading: *Celebration Day Farewell Costume Party! Free Booze & Food, Music,* he relaxed; a little.

Captain Hook in his formal Scottish gear watched the small black cavalcade approach; he had sent off Manhandle, Marie and Millie into town in his limo to establish alibis. 'Park outside the Sheriff's office if need be.'

On arrival at the castle, the drivers and the limo chauffeur stood at attention holding the doors open as the VIP signatories and others disembarked.

'Are you, my dear, Captain Hook?' said the Asian man leading from the front in a beautifully cut dark Italian Armani suit, stiff white wing collared shirt and a crimson silk bowtie.

'What pleasure to meet your flesh at last,' said Mr Chew, extending a well-manicured hand with gold rings on every finger. The left one for delicacy, Rick noticed.

'You are most welcome Mr Chew.' Giving a formal bow. Mr Chew nodded back with his trademark smug smile on his otherwise inscrutable face. They shook hands.

'I must admire your proposition, Captain,' said Mr Chew as he was led with the others through the open doors of the Castle.

'Splendid, splendid,' said Mr Chew as if to himself and swiftly looking around taking it all in. Others followed, some wide-eyed, some slowly nodding their heads wisely in approval. A group wandered about with mouths agape. A small weasel-like woman with a mink stole over her shoulders studied the plans above the business table and smacked her lips while rubbing her hands together. There was universal approval. Game, set and match, thought Captain Rick Hook.

Standing on a small dais, Hook welcomed the guests and gave a short speech about the merits of the proposal and what a delight it was to have such a wonderful opportunity to place it before such a knowledgeable gathering and lauding their vision for being here. White bow-tied waiters went to and fro distributing champagne. Rick apologised for the upstairs areas being out of bounds. 'Starting upgrading, a small matter of safety,' he said, 'but you can see a lot from here and you have all seen the plans and were free to gaze on or walk the delightful grounds.' On this early sultry evening, all the ground floor doors were open including the fire doors and all the windows. Mr Chew then gave a short return speech of gratitude and invited the assembly to clap with him, which they did with enthusiasm.

'Pleased to follow his example and sign,' requested Mr Chew. All complied after Mr Chew made a great show of signing first. Captain Hook raised his eyebrows at Mr Chew, a prearranged signal; who turned to his hovering secretary and gave her a nod. She immediately pulled out her iPhone and began to punch in numbers and letters transferring a huge hunk of Conglomerate and Chew's own money into Hook's purposely set up bank account, the new balance consequently went swiftly straight into his secret personal Swiss account. Captain Hook approached Mr Chew more closely.

'Mr Chew, you are now the owner of this castle and I, your guest.'

Mr Chew bowed graciously. 'Long may that be so, Captain.'

Captain Hook invited them all to dine, which they did, extolling the fare, especially the fresh crab. 'Only just caught today, from our own Charity Point on the coast,' said the straight-faced Captain. Captain Hook wandered around explaining this and that, expounding the history of the Castle, what was happening upstairs and such and so forth, then made his apologies he was going to his study for a short time to make the documents secure. Back in no time, he said while placing the documents in his calfskin satchel, one of his favourite possessions. He then departed waving his hook. Through a hidden door, he ran to a grassy knoll and looked down. There she was, his plane idling on the long fairway, it was glowing silver in the late afternoon sun. He returned to the castle wall and carefully lit the fuse that wound up a water downpipe to the upper floors and roof. He and Manhandle had spent hours grouping whiskey bottles from the cellar into every upstairs room. Connected to the bottles and the roof beams was what looked like a white electric extension cord was in fact high explosive Cortex cord procured from Manhandles Army buddy. The Cortex eventually led to a powerful detonator and from there to the fifteen-minute fuse which Rick had just lit outside.

Without hurry, Rick walked down to his jet and was welcomed aboard by his pilot. 'Great to see you again, sir,' said the pilot with a wide grin.

'Likewise, Bill, long time no see. Let's get the hell out of here,' replied Rick stashing the satchel and going through to the back with Sarah giving her a quick kiss. With a whistle, the plane ran down the golf fairway and into the clear gathering twilight sky. The explosions below came as one and the upper floors burst into incandescent fire. People could be seen fleeing outside and spilling onto the grounds in panic then standing around in groups looking up at their disappearing dreams and all by himself, one Mr Chew.

'Farewell prison, goodbye past.' Laughed Rick.

Sarah was enthralled with the flames leaping and jumping into the sky. Rick went forward and told the pilot to dive and bank to the left, something was going on down there in the countryside which turned out to be a large melee of cars tearing away from a large barn in all directions even some through fences, one squashed itself against a lone tree, another ran into a creek. The Sheriff's car hurtling from the opposite direction, red and blue lights flashing was pushed unceremoniously off the road almost up to its roof in the foul bog in the headlong rush; through a side window, a black-gloved hand fired a .44 wildly into the sky. *The last bit of Peninsular type lunacy to see them off,* thought Rick. Below the Castle's upper floors collapsed eventually onto the lower and fresh fires started. The pilot levelled off and then climbed and settled down to cruising speed and altitude. Rick locked the cabin door. Sarah and Rick then relaxed. *So this is the real deal,* they both thought simultaneously raising their champagne glasses in harmony, in a salute to success.

THE END